Summer Sandcastle

Summer Sandcastle

LYNNE SCOTT-DRENNAN

DOUBLEDAY & COMPANY, INC.

GARDEN CITY, NEW YORK

1984

All of the characters in this book
are fictitious, and any resemblance
to actual persons, living or dead,
is purely coincidental.

Library of Congress Cataloging in Publication Data

Scott-Drennan, Lynne.
Summer sandcastle.

I. Title.
PS3569.C695S9 1984   813'.54   83–16613
ISBN 0-385-19234-7

Summer Sandcastle

CHAPTER 1

With exaggerated care, as though hoping not to break a spell, Kendall Blake set the phone gently back in its cradle, tucked a stray wisp of raven hair neatly behind her ear, and looked across their two desks at Meg Potter.

"Meg," she said slowly, her dark, gray green eyes gleaming with excitement, "that was Stephen Langston's office. I think we may have hit the jackpot."

Her petite blond partner stared at her unbelievingly. "Stephen Langston?"

"*The* Stephen Langston. Of Langston Industries. At least," she corrected, "*the* Stephen Langston's executive assistant—a Miss Hutton."

"And he . . . she . . . wants us?"

Kendall nodded. "Mr. Langston has decided to refurbish the Sandcastle," she said, her husky voice taking on the professional tones of a great man's aide as she mimicked the caller. "He has heard many excellent things about Blake and Potter and has seen some of the results of their work for himself. He would like Miss Blake to come out early this afternoon for a preliminary consultation."

"Just like that? No bids, no estimates?" Meg's blue eyes were wide.

"Just like that. I started to explain how we do things, but she was very brisk. Just said she understood all that and would look forward to meeting me."

"Good gracious! But where do you suppose someone like Stephen Langston has seen our work?"

Kendall didn't hesitate. "It has to be your Aunt Hilda. He lives in Pebble Beach, and her house is the only one that we've done there. Besides, she knows everyone and is always entertaining. And she talks incessantly about what marvelous things we accomplished in her drab little abode."

"Dear Aunt Hilda." Meg grinned at Kendall's irreverence toward the elegant little house in the Del Monte Forest. "But it might just as easily have been someone here. We *have* done several homes of prominent people."

A wry twinkle lit Kendall's eyes. "I suppose you can technically refer to three homes as 'several,' " she conceded. "But I hardly think that a member of the Carmel school board, a locally prominent artist, or a summer resident who hasn't set foot in his house since we finished it can be counted as likely acquaintances for someone like Stephen Langston."

"No, I guess not," Meg agreed. "But it might have been someone else, someone whose wardrobe or colors you've done or a client who just wanted help with a kitchen or something. It needn't be one of the few who's had the whole package, you know."

"Call your Aunt Hilda," Kendall suggested. "I'd bet on what the results will be, but it would be fiendish to take your money so easily."

Meg's only response was to reach for the phone on her desk. Kendall watched as she began to dial the familiar number, then leaned back in her chair with a small sigh of satisfaction. It didn't really matter who had recommended their services. To have landed a big fish like Langston was a coup indeed for Blake and Potter.

She glanced around the studio's office-reception room, tastefully furnished with quiet blue-and-gray elegance. Strategically placed lush green potted plants, including a magnificent Boston fern hanging in the window, gave the place an unexpected touch of hominess, besides providing conversational gambits for new clients. Meg was the one with the green thumb. Kendall turned her thoughts fondly to the vivaciously pretty girl at the other desk. How interesting life had become since that luncheon in San Francisco!

It had started as the usual thing—two college friends who

hadn't seen each other for a while agreeing to meet at the Iron Horse in Maiden Lane for lunch. Kendall had been working for one of the larger department stores on Union Square, and Meg had just finished eighteen months of studying advanced interior design in Paris. Over salad and deliciously crisp Monte Cristo sandwiches, she had explained that she wanted to open her own studio on the Monterey Peninsula, where both girls had grown up.

"Hey, girl, stop daydreaming." Kendall realized that she had been staring blankly at her friend and now focused her eyes properly. Meg, having hung up the phone, tossed her blond curls and grinned at her again. "You were right. It was Aunt Hilda. What were you thinking about right then?"

"San Francisco." Kendall answered the question automatically, although she didn't as a rule like people to pry into her private thoughts. But Meg could no more help such questions than she could help breathing. They had been roommates for a time at school, and the first month or so had nearly driven Kendall crazy until she realized that Meg was like a friendly puppy—curious, perfectly harmless, and totally gregarious. From that point on, she had focused on her friend's good points and had learned to accept the inevitable questions with graceful resignation.

"Do you miss the city?" Meg asked now.

"Good grief, no. I loved it, but I was lonely and bored, and I hated that stupid job I'd gotten myself locked into."

"Cosmetics analyst," Meg breathed in tones of exaggerated admiration.

"Slavery," Kendall corrected. "If you think it's fun to slap makeup on bored housewives all day, every day, you simply can't have considered the matter. But then I took that color class, thinking it would help me choose the right tones for my customers to wear, and I got hooked."

"I'll say you did!" Meg laughed, her blue eyes twinkling merrily. "That day at the Iron Horse, when you suddenly launched into your spiel on the marvelous benefits of having one's personal colors matched to one's hair, skin, and eye tones, I thought I would die of boredom before you tired of the subject. I mean, it wasn't as though I didn't have some small notion of proper color combinations before that."

Kendall's rare smile lit her face. "I know. I must have sounded so ridiculously naive, as though I were daring to tell you your business."

Meg chuckled. "Well, maybe it wasn't that bad. I was hardly an established designer, and you did teach me quite a lot about personalizing colors once I really began to listen. Besides, I was looking for some sort of gimmick that would set me apart from all the others here. Then, we both seemed to have the same scathingly brilliant idea at the same time."

"We may have both thought of it at the same time," Kendall said quietly, "but it's a good thing you were the one to put it into words. I'd never have been so bold as to pretend that my skills matched yours."

"Rot," was the cordial response. "You've never been one to hide your light under a bushel, Miss Blake. You knew exactly how good you were. Not only had you taken every sort of color class imaginable by then, but you also had the benefit of having read everything you could get your hands on on the subject, and you had studied such mundane things as wardrobe management and closet organization and so forth, besides. They sounded pretty dull when you wrote about them, but when you started speaking, and your eyes lit up, I was interested in spite of myself. Then came the brilliant idea, and here we are."

Yes, Kendall thought, there they were, in an elegant little studio just off Ocean Avenue in Carmel. The discreet lettering on the window read:

BLAKE AND POTTER
FOUR SEASONS COLOR MANAGEMENT
INTERIOR DESIGN

Their plan had been a simple one. Kendall would first analyze the client's personal color needs; then, armed with that information, Meg would develop suggestions for decorating, redecorating, or whatever was needed, while Kendall took on the client's wardrobe organization and storage needs. They worked together, but the ultimate design was Meg's. Consequently, Kendall had balked at first when Meg had suggested that she get top billing.

"Nonsense," Meg had said crisply. "I'd never have had the idea at all if it hadn't been for you, and you put just as much money into this studio as I did. Besides, you're the one the client will meet first, and I think we should do all we can to show him that getting the colors right is the most important part of the service we offer. I can coordinate design and color and come up with a brilliantly decorated room—if I do say so myself. But the client might hate it. I had more than one experience in Paris where my professor would like something and a visitor would say it was awful. Monsieur Lapin always said that only meant the visitor had no taste, but it could just as well have been that he didn't like the colors. And you know as well as I do that letting the client select his own colors without any guidance from us can be absolutely catastrophic. But he—or she, as the case may be—can do it if we know ahead of time that when he says blue, if he's a summer type, he means a grayed blue and not turquoise or royal. With that sort of ammunition, we can go ahead full steam."

Kendall had smiled then at Meg's unconscious use of the seasonal term to describe their theoretical client. It had taken a while to convince her that categorizing colors by the seasons—a method devised by New York color consultant and author Carole Jackson—made communication easier, but once Meg had been convinced, the terms came as easily to her as they did to Kendall. And it was Meg who had bought the little brass plaque to hang on the wall. It read quite simply: "To every Thing there is a Season," and the words had, to all intents and purposes, become their motto.

Kendall had pointed out that they would never have found their choice little studio if it hadn't been for Aunt Hilda, who was after all Meg's aunt, but Meg had capped the argument by saying that Aunt Hilda would be perfectly happy to adopt Kendall, too, and that was that. That had been more than six months ago, and they had not done badly since. In fact, thanks to Aunt Hilda and her numerous contacts, they had done rather well. They could even afford the services of Sally Hunt, the part-time office assistant who answered their phone, took messages, and did other assorted odd jobs, although they had not yet attained such heights that they could afford to employ a fully skilled secretary. It occurred to Kendall now that a client like Stephen Langston would provide them with an opportunity to reach those heights more quickly than they had anticipated.

"What else did Aunt Hilda say?"

Meg wrinkled her pug little nose, trying to remember the gist of her aunt's loquacious conversation. "She said she thought he would be exactly right for you," she began with a teasing smile. "I expect that's because of his money." Kendall made no response, merely waiting with exaggerated politeness for Meg to continue. Aunt Hilda made a steady habit of trying to pair her favorite niece and her niece's best friend up with eligible gentlemen. Meg's smile blossomed into a full-fledged grin. "More to the point perhaps, she also said he was at one of her parties and complimented the decor. That's her favorite opening, you know, and I guess she did her usual snow job on the poor man, though I'd have thought he'd be a bit more difficult as a target than the sort she's used to."

"Give her credit," Kendall retorted with amusement. "Your Aunt Hilda could talk the spots off a leopard and make him think he was giving only his fair share."

Meg laughed. "You're right, of course, but I still think she has outdone herself this time."

Privately agreeing, Kendall returned a light response and began to check through the leather satchel containing the necessities of her craft, which she would take with her on the jaunt to Pebble Beach. Then she stepped into the tiny powder room to check her own appearance. After straightening the bow at the neck of her white blouse and dragging a comb through her smooth, dark, shoulder-length hair, she decided it would do. Her lipstick still looked fresh enough. That was one thing about the new, bright colors. They stayed. The deep, wine red shade was very becoming to her, and the color was picked up again in the trace of rouge high on her prominent cheekbones. Her skin was pale, almost milky, but with a translucence to it that, along with the dark hair and large, black-fringed eyes, gave her a resemblance—noted early in her school career by teasing classmates—to Snow White.

Kendall had detested the resemblance and had done what she could to offset it by conscientiously schooling her features into perpetual inscrutability. It had required a good deal of emotional control, since she was not exactly cool or reserved by nature, but she decided that, her looks being what they were, she would prefer to be thought mysterious rather than friendly and outgoing. Now, after years of constant practice, the attitude was habitual. Her dark, gray green eyes had a piercing quality that added to the illusion, often giving the impression that she could read one's mind without giving away a single thought of her own. People meeting her for the first time tended to think her aloof, even snobbish, and Meg had once confided that she had feared such an impression might frighten off prospective clients. So far, however, it had proven to be more of an asset than a disadvantage. It gave her a solid, professional air that more than compensated for her awe-inspiring beauty.

Kendall knew she was beautiful. She had very few illusions about herself. In fact, if pressed to do so, she could give a generally objective list of her faults and virtues. She knew, for example, that her eyes and complexion were her best features, closely followed by her hair and figure, and that her nose—a trifle too large for perfection—and her mouth—too wide—were her worst. Words such as glamorous, seductive, and exotic had often been employed to describe her, and she believed they were probably apt. But she could also be over-bearing, sarcastic, and intolerant to the point of contempt.

And her temper sometimes had an alarming tendency to fly beyond her control.

She was not proud of these last characteristics, and she did what she could to subdue them, but her sometimes brutal honesty tended to get the best of any good intentions. She was not tactful by nature, as Meg was. In fact, whatever she knew about tact had been hard-learned through sometimes bitter experience. Nevertheless, she had to make a conscious effort whenever tact was called for not to say the first thing that came to mind; and it had occurred to her upon more than one occasion that it would have been a much more comfortable world for all concerned if those who could not tolerate an honest answer did not ask leading questions.

With a final *moue* at her reflection, she gathered her things and said good-bye to Meg. A short time later, as she carefully guided her yellow Camaro out of its tiny parking place and down the narrow street to Ocean Avenue, Meg's comment about Stephen Langston came back to her. It *was* odd that someone like that would want Blake and Potter. One would think he'd be more likely to call upon a well-established firm, to go for the showplace rather than the personal approach they offered. But it would not do to speculate at this point. She would have to wait and see.

Taking the first opportunity that offered, she bulldozed her way into the intersection, knowing that despite the presence of four-way stop signs, there was no point whatsoever in waiting for someone to let her through. In Carmel, one simply drove assertively and hoped for the best. Usually, it worked out fine.

She turned left and headed slowly down the tree-lined hill toward the beach, marveling that she could still feel a sense of wonder at the beauty of the little town. Carmel, despite its battles against encroaching hippies during the sixties and other odd tribes since, still retained its villagelike appearance, its old-fashioned flavor. It was probably one of the most commercially minded burgs in the country, but it didn't look it. There wasn't a modern-looking, glass-and-steel structure in the town. Even the gas stations retained an old-world look. Some went a little far, in fact, like the one built of quarry stones and made to resemble a tiny medieval fortress. But that, too, was the essence of Carmel. Anyone had a right to use his own imagination to do his own thing, so long as he didn't clash with the elemental nature of the place.

She turned onto San Antonio Avenue and drove past huge, tree-shaded homes to the City Gate, where she stopped to give her name to the guard and to tell him that she was expected at the Sandcastle. He checked his clipboard, then motioned her through with a smile. It gave her the usual smug sense of satisfaction to be entering Del Monte Forest without paying the four-dollar fee required of visitors to the Seventeen-Mile Drive. She wondered if the inhabitants of the forest retained that sense for long, or if they just grew accustomed to it. They didn't even have to stop at the gates, of course, for they had numbered identification tags for their cars. Imagine stopping one of the Crosby family or Clint or Maggie Eastwood to demand proper identification! She smiled to herself at the thought.

Following what was now Carmel Avenue uphill to the Seventeen-Mile Drive itself, then turning onto Sunridge, she found herself wondering again what Stephen Langston would be like. She could not remember having ever seen a picture of the man, but she imagined that, to have reached the height of his profession as he had done, he must be in his late forties or early fifties. He was practically a legend, after all, and legends did not generally feature men in their twenties. Not in the world of big business anyway.

She tried to remember just what it was that Langston Industries manufactured. There were numerous marine supply outlets in the area that were connected one way or another with Langston, but the local company was part of an international conglomerate, and surely it didn't deal only in marine supplies. There was that new factory that had been built in one of the old canneries on Cannery Row, but she had no idea what was produced there. She did know she had been im-

pressed that they had retained the character of the cannery
when they rebuilt. Everyone had grumped and moaned
when the permits were approved, thinking that Langston
would destroy the whole Row by putting in a smoke-belch-
ing, noise-making cracker box of corrugated steel; however,
if one did not know it was there, one would never think the
building to be a factory at all. But what sort of man—

Firmly, Kendall told herself that she was speculating again
and that it could do no possible good. She passed the little
lane that led up to Aunt Hilda's house and decided that once
she had finished the consultation with Langston she would
drop in for a short visit. Aunt Hilda, knowing she had driven
into the forest, would never forgive her if she did not stop
long enough for a cup of tea and a cigarette, as well as an
exchange of views on Blake and Potter's latest client.

A moment later, she caught sight of the two tall stone
pillars supporting the heavy steel gates that normally shut
the Sandcastle off from the rest of the world. Matching brass
plaques on either pillar were labeled Sandcastle, and Langston. Very neat, she thought. Very unassuming. No large Be-
ware of Dog sign like half the homes in the area displayed. No
Protected Premises or No Trespassing signs. Just the two
small plaques. The gates were invitingly open, but when she
turned the Camaro onto the gravel drive and drove between
them, they slowly began to shut behind her, and she knew
that the premises were well guarded despite the lack of any
outward sign. It gave her a rather eerie sensation to know
that somewhere someone was watching her, but it was forgotten almost immediately as the Sandcastle loomed into
sight ahead of her.

Constructed of smooth, gray stone in the Scotch baronial
tradition, it truly looked like a well-built sandcastle that had
been settled in amongst the lofty Monterey pine and cypress
trees. Stone steps that led up to the steel-banded, heavy
timber front door were flanked by two large rhododendron
bushes, but there had been no other attempt to improve
upon Mother Nature's landscaping skills.

A deliciously woodsy smell greeted her as she climbed out of the car, adjusted her shoulder bag, and hefted the leather satchel. Her feet crunched on the gravel. She glanced around, wondering why she felt no sense of awe at being in such a place. There didn't seem to be a soul around, except for the telltale orange flash of a tanager flitting from one tree and the harsh screech of a stellar jay offering undoubtedly rude opinions of the world from another. But she felt perfectly comfortable, as though she had been here many times before. The sensation was even eerier than that caused by the unseen watcher.

She approached the front door looking for the doorbell, but just as she was reaching to push it, the door opened, and a black-and-white-clad maid smiled cheerfully at her.

"Miss Blake?"

"Yes," said Kendall. "To see Mr. Langston."

"Of course, ma'am. Just step in and make yourself comfortable. I'll tell Miss Hutton that you've arrived."

"Thank you." Kendall watched the maid cross the parquet floor with the sound of rustling taffeta, then glanced around at the entry hall. It was just as one might have expected, medieval in flavor but comfortable too. There was an overstuffed settee against one wall, and she moved with slow deliberation toward it, her eyes drifting from a large coat of arms high on the wall above it to the various land- and seascapes that adorned the other walls. There was little coordination of design here, just a collection of things the owner probably liked. She wondered if the rest of the place would be the same. She wondered also how Meg would feel about redecorating a castle.

It seemed as though she had no sooner sat down than the maid returned with a tall, slim young woman in a well-tailored, rust-colored suit, whose most arresting feature was a mane of honey gold hair cut in a long and very becoming shag. Kendall stood up, and the clear hazel eyes candidly appraising her sharpened noticeably.

"How do you do, Miss Blake? I am Sylvia Hutton, Mr. Langston's assistant. Will you follow me, please?"

Kendall nodded coolly, and Miss Hutton turned back the way she had come, only to pause again when the maid spoke. "Excuse me, Miss Hutton, but will you be requiring coffee or tea?"

"Coffee, Charlotte, for three, in the study," Miss Hutton replied briskly. "Come along, Miss Blake."

Her placid expression revealing none of the resentment that was rapidly building within her at the other young woman's somewhat officious attitude, Kendall followed. They passed out of the entry hall into a short corridor and turned left almost immediately into a large, book-lined room containing a heavy leather sofa and matching chair, a large, untidy leather-topped desk, and a smaller walnut desk with a typewriter on it. Miss Hutton motioned Kendall to the sofa and took the matching chair for herself.

"Mr. Langston seems to have stepped out for a moment, Miss Blake, but he will return shortly. You might tell me about yourself while we wait."

"What would you like to know?" Kendall inquired with her customary reserve.

"All about you, of course," declared the other. "I have been placed in charge of this project of Steve's, and I should like to know all there is to know about you and Miss Potter before we proceed." She made the project sound slightly tiresome, as though it ought to be over and done as quickly as possible so that she might get on to other, more important things.

"You told me earlier that Mr. Langston had seen and approved our work," Kendall said in a carefully even tone. "I cannot imagine what else it would be your business to know."

"It would perhaps be best if you were to allow me to be the judge of that," responded Miss Hutton crushingly. "You might begin by telling me where you went to school."

Kendall decided that she was face-to-face with an assertive, probably ambitious woman who was trying to get the upper hand at the outset, and who, for some reason, considered her to be a challenge. The thought brought a glint of amusement to her eye.

"I have more than one degree," she said gently, "but no sort of diploma that particularly qualifies me for this sort of task. If degrees impress you, Miss Potter has whole walls covered with the appropriate sort. However, Mr. Langston is hiring our talent, not bits of sheepskin, and the success of our work must depend upon his satisfaction with it and nothing else. Now, Miss Hutton, I should like to meet Mr. Langston as soon as possible. My time is limited, as I'm sure you must be aware, for your own cannot but be the same. So, if you don't mind—"

A tinge of extra color had crept into Miss Hutton's face as Kendall spoke, and although she retained her outer composure, her next words came a bit stiffly. "I fear that perhaps you do not fully appreciate the situation, Miss Blake. Mr. Langston will certainly be paying your fees, but you will be working directly under my supervision, so it would be best for all concerned if you do not begin our association by being obstructive."

Kendall stood up, her steady, disdainful gaze pinning Miss Hutton to the chair. She spoke slowly, but her tone was distinctly frosty. "I am afraid that there has been an error. When I offered to explain our procedures over the phone, Miss Hutton, you refused, saying that you already understood them. Therefore, you must know that a preliminary consultation includes a color analysis and a view of the premises, with a subsequent discussion of the specific requirements for the job. It does not entail an impertinent inquiry into my personal life or background." She gathered up her purse and satchel and moved purposefully toward the door.

Miss Hutton began to speak rather quickly, but Kendall was too angry to listen. Meg would be disappointed, of course, even angry, but there was nothing she could do about that. The woman was impossible. There would be a continual clash between them, and neither she nor Meg could work under such conditions.

With outward dignity, she reached for the doorknob, but before she could grasp it, the door opened suddenly, making her take a quick step backward in order to avoid being struck. Then, glancing up, she went perfectly still, feeling as though she had been struck after all.

There before her stood one of the largest, handsomest men she had ever seen in her life. He had to be at least six feet five inches tall, she decided, and his shoulders seemed as broad as a barn. Chiseled features in a well-bronzed face gave him the exact sort of rugged good looks she liked best. Then, while she was still struggling to catch her breath, twinkling sea blue eyes met hers, and she received an even greater shock.

It was as though she knew him, had known him all her life. The feeling was similar to that which she had had about the house, only deeper, not just a sense of familiarity, but a sense of intimacy. This man was going to be important to her, no . . . he was going to be indispensable to her future happiness.

Unsuccessfully, she tried to suppress what certainly must be the absurd exaggerations of an unstable mind. She had never seen the man before; therefore, she told herself firmly, such feelings were not only incomprehensible but utterly ridiculous. Why then, would they not dissipate? He, too, seemed stunned, but that was no doubt the result of nearly running her down, and he recovered more quickly, grinning and looking past her at Miss Hutton, who had jumped speedily to her feet.

"Sylvia!" he boomed in a deep baritone. "What are you doing in here, and why the devil didn't you tell me that Miss Blake had arrived?"

Miss Hutton retained her poise, but Kendall thought she detected a slight glint of wariness in the hazel eyes before it was blinked away. "I thought we'd find you here, Steve," she said smoothly. "When we didn't, I assumed you had just stepped out briefly and would return."

Langston chuckled. "My fault," he said lightly, turning his gaze back to Kendall. "How do you do, Miss Blake? We usually do conduct all our business matters in here, so I can scarcely blame my efficient Sylvia. Just thought it a shame to hide you away in this back slum when you could be feasting your eyes on our view from the living room. Come along with me. You come, too, Sylvia. When Charlotte told me where you were, I told her to bring the refreshments out there. If it weren't for the blasted wind, we could have it on the patio."

He turned abruptly, clearly certain that they would follow; and, feeling much as though the wind had been knocked out of her, Kendall trailed meekly after him, all thought of departure gone. She scarcely heeded Miss Hutton's presence behind her. All her attention was focused upon the great man himself.

He couldn't be more than thirty-five, she thought. He didn't really even look that old. Moreover, he was a gorgeous hunk of male animal if ever she had seen one. And she had probably seen more than her share.

There had been men in her life as long as she could remember, but not one of them had ever stirred her senses once during an entire acquaintance the way this one had done in the mere twinkling of an eye. Certainly, Jack Susmann, presently her most frequent escort, had never done so. And Jack, the son of a wealthy Peninsula automobile dealer, was handsome and charming enough to turn most young women's heads. She was probably being silly, she told herself, watching Langston stride through the Gothic archway ahead of her. He had merely startled her. That was all. Then why did her insides still feel like so much jelly?

CHAPTER 2

None of Kendall's feelings showed in her face, of course, and she thanked her fates that she had learned to school her expression so well, for if she had ever needed command over herself, she needed it now. They entered a huge room, and through a far wall that seemed to consist entirely of glass, the view, just as Langston had promised, was magnificent—an expanse of sand and sea broken only by the occasional cypress or pine, or the jutting of dark gray, rough-pointed rocks. She drew in an appreciative breath.

"Fabulous, isn't it?" demanded that low-pitched, almost melodious voice. He spoke more quietly now, and she forced herself to face him squarely, little realizing for once how calmly poised she appeared.

"It is a lovely view, Mr. Langston. But as I was telling Miss Hutton, my time is extremely limited, and I shall need to see the entire house once I have completed the color analysis. So perhaps we might get started as quickly as possible. If you will sit over there by the window where the light is best, we can begin."

The boyish grin flashed out again. "Sure, Miss Blake. I like your style. All business. I'm like that myself, I can tell you. No pussyfooting around. Pour the coffee, Sylvia. How do you want me, ma'am?"

She arranged a chair, then pulled up an occasional table and set her large mirror upon it, tilting it so that he could see himself. Next, she withdrew a large white cloth from her satchel and draped it around his shoulders. "This is so your eye won't be fooled by the colors you're already wearing, Mr. Langston." Her tone was matter-of-fact, but she was thinking that she could scarcely improve upon the outfit he had chosen for himself. He was wearing a charcoal gray three-piece suit with a creamy white shirt and a light blue tie that nearly matched his eyes. With his dark brown hair, heavy dark brows, and tremendous size, the outfit was perhaps a bit intimidating, but he looked magnificent in it, nevertheless.

She stepped back to assure herself that everything was as it should be, and that twinkling gaze intercepted hers once more. She forced herself to meet it squarely, but her heart began to pound in a most uncharacteristic way. Maybe this was what people meant when they talked about a magnetic personality, she reflected. Maybe it was just a case of the man's having an incredible charisma. But whatever it was, Kendall knew she would have to watch her step if she wanted to maintain that cool reserve she had worked so long and so hard to perfect. Firmly, she pinned her thoughts to the task at hand.

She knew by looking at him that Stephen Langston would fall into the summer category. The sunlight through the window picked up auburn highlights in the dark hair that might have fooled someone less experienced into mistaking him for winter or even autumn, but the pink color in his cheeks and the bright, sky blue eyes told Kendall all she really needed to know.

His skin showed blue undertones despite his deep tan, and his eyes were of an intensity and purity of color that could go with no other category. But he must see for himself, of course, so she began with her usual explanation as she set out the large squares of material she used for her comparisons.

"I do this by seasonal categories, Mr. Langston, but that is only because it seems to help our clients understand the elements of color selection better. The first thing we want is to determine whether you will belong to a warm or cool season."

"I'm a cool customer," he quipped.

"You're joking, sir," she replied mildly, "but as it happens, you're quite right. Look at the difference." She spread a large square of navy blue under his chin, then replaced it with a dark brown, trying to maintain her businesslike demeanor despite the nearly electric tension she felt as a result of his nearness. "Which is better?" It seemed odd to her that the words came with their usual calm.

"The blue," he replied decisively. "That was easy. Brown is for hicks and midwestern businessmen. Wouldn't be caught dead in it myself."

"Well, you shouldn't wear that shade of brown at any rate," she agreed, amused in spite of her disordered senses, "though I don't know that I agree with you about hicks. A rose brown—"

"No browns." He shook his head.

"Very well." She removed the dark brown square and set it aside, steadier now. "Perhaps it would help if you understood what to look for before we continue."

"It would, at that." His twinkling eyes met hers in the mirror, and Kendall firmly suppressed the tingling sensation that seemed to creep up from her very toes, curling them in their black T-strapped, high-heeled sandals.

"The right color will smooth and define your facial planes," she said briskly. Her speech was clipped now, her sentences brief. "You want to watch your face, not the color swatch. If the color is wrong, your tan will look muddy or pale. You'll notice lines at your eyes and mouth. You'll look older."

"We wouldn't want that, would we?" he said quietly.

"No, sir. We want you to look healthy and alive."

"He hardly looks dead now," contributed Miss Hutton, watching them skeptically over her coffee cup.

"Just ignore Sylvia," Langston said briefly, his eyes disconcertingly on Kendall again. "She thinks this part of the project is silly. But I've seen where your talents lead, Miss Blake, so play on."

"Yes, sir." Quickly, she showed him other color combinations that clearly placed him within the summer spectrum. He even agreed that rose brown was an acceptable color when she smilingly pointed out that an expensive leather or suede jacket in that shade would scarcely label its wearer a hick. But when she removed the orange swatch that Langston said made him look like a yellow-fever victim and replaced it with one of powder pink, the blue eyes flashed.

"Take that away," he growled.

"But, Mr. Langston, it's only a comparison! Just see how the pink softens—"

"Take the damn thing away!" His temper flared so quickly that Kendall looked at him in astonishment, though she managed to reply coolly enough.

"Of course I'll put it away, but I thought you understood that my intent is only to—"

"I don't give a damn for your intent. I don't wear pink! I'm a hard-nosed businessman, Miss Blake, not a flaming fa—"

"Steve!" Miss Hutton had risen to refill her cup and now shot him a teasing smile, but Kendall noted that glint of wariness again as well. "Really, Steve, what will she think of you? Shall I warm up your coffee, or would you prefer a drink?"

Langston opened his mouth to bellow his answer, but then his eyes met Kendall's cool, rather amused gaze in the mirror, and he shut it again.

"Shall we continue, Mr. Langston?"

His expression relaxed. "My apologies, Miss Blake. Sylvia, you can get me some more coffee. It's too early yet for anything stronger." He turned back to Kendall. "Did I say I was a cool customer? I'm afraid you've discovered my temper rather early in the game, but I must say, I applaud your calm. I've got secretaries who turn tail and run when I bellow like that."

"I am not a secretary, Mr. Langston, and in my time, I have dealt successfully with tempers far more violent than yours." She remembered some of the *grandes dames* amongst her San Francisco customers. One or two could easily have made mincemeat of Mr. Langston's comparatively paltry temper. There was that time she had tactlessly suggested an eye cream that would help to minimize Miss Van Walder's deepening crow's-feet. And despite her words to the contrary, she had not always dealt well with such situations. Even now, something deep within her quailed at the memory of the august Miss Van Walder's fiery rage. But Langston's sudden flash of temper had not alarmed her. Indeed, she had been far more disturbed by his smiles.

He had grimaced at her chilly tone, but now he looked at her through narrowed eyes. "Perhaps you have at that," he said slowly. However, he didn't pursue the matter. "What do we do now?"

"We examine the summer palette to determine your best basic and accessory colors. Afterward, if you like, I can help you check through your wardrobe for things that are already suitable, as well as for gaps. I don't know yet which of our services you want to utilize. As you know if you talked with Hilda Quick, we offer a fairly wide range. Miss Hutton explained that you wish to refurbish the house, but—"

"But you could also refurbish me, right?"

"Yes, if you like," Kendall replied. She had herself well in hand once more, and she treated him to another of her cool, direct gazes.

"My time is limited, Miss Blake, and I certainly have no time for shopping expeditions. I leave most of that to Sylvia, I'm afraid."

"We offer a shopping service, Mr. Langston," she said, glancing at the other young woman and thinking that she didn't seem the sort to relish being sent on shopping expeditions. Her steady gaze returned to Langston. "Once I have examined your wardrobe and made a list of your specific needs, I simply take the list and the color swatches, and I can do the whole thing in an afternoon. We deal directly with Magnin's, Dick Bruhn's, and many other shops all over the Peninsula. If you like, we can arrange to leave your measurements and a palette with your best colors marked at any store you choose. Then, if you need a shirt, a tie, or even an entire outfit, a phone call from you, Miss Hutton, or even your secretary will soon accomplish your purpose."

"Sounds terrific. Let's get to it."

Willingly, Kendall reached for her satchel to get the palette of summer swatches, but before she had begun to lay them out, the door from the hallway opened and a young, curly-headed, bespectacled gentleman in a light tweed suit quick-stepped into the room.

"Steve!" He glanced uncertainly at the white sheet around Langston's shoulders and then at Kendall. "That is . . . Mr. Langston, the car is waiting. You'll be late if you don't step on it, sir."

"Late for what?"

The young man hesitated again, then gave a sigh of patient resignation. "The dentist, sir. Two-thirty. You can just make it."

The color in Langston's cheeks deepened, but when he spoke, his voice was crisp, controlled. "Cancel it."

The young man glanced helplessly at Miss Hutton, but she returned only a tiny, enigmatic smile. His gaze darted back to Langston, and he seemed to square his shoulders. "I can't do that."

"Why not?" Langston barked.

"Your orders, sir," the young man said staunchly. "Besides, Dr. Morrissy moved heaven and earth to squeeze you in today. Next time, he'll more 'n likely tell us both to go to the devil."

"Damn it, Jerry, can't you see I'm busy!" The quick temper had flared again, but Jerry met those blazing eyes without flinching.

"Yes, sir, but the car is waiting, and if I were such a numb-skull as to cancel this appointment, you'd want my head on a platter the next time you sit down to eat, and you know it."

Langston glared at him, but the flash of temper was over. "You're right. It's just that going to the dentist is such a pain in the—" He broke off with a rueful glance at Kendall. "Forget it, Jerry. Sorry I snapped."

"Never mind, sir," the younger man grinned. "It wasn't nearly as bad as I'd anticipated."

"Oh, it wasn't, was it! You'll be giving Miss Blake a wonderful notion of my character if I don't get you out of here *tout de suite.*" He got to his feet, pulling the sheet away and handing it to Kendall. "Sorry about this, Miss Blake. I didn't realize we'd taken so long. If it were a mere international oil merger, I'd put it off, but one doesn't dare offend one's dentist."

"That's quite all right, Mr. Langston," Kendall said, her surface calm battling to conceal a surge of disappointment that seemed altogether out of proportion to the situation. She began to gather her things. "We can always schedule another appointment for you, and in the meantime, I'm certain Miss Hutton can show me over the house and explain just what sort of changes you want to make."

"Of course she can. It's been a pleasure to make your acquaintance." He held out a hand, and Kendall found her own clasped firmly. She glanced up into his eyes and met a warm look quite different from the mischievous twinkle that generally seemed to lurk there. It was unexpected, and to her astonishment, it nearly undid her. She felt as though she were being caressed. She could not drag her gaze from his. It was as though she were mesmerized, under some sort of spell, while the warmth of his look seemed to spread through her entire body. Then young Jerry cleared his throat impatiently and the mood was broken. Langston glanced at him, then turned back to Kendall. "You just tell Sylvia what you want, and she'll see to it." She nodded, not trusting herself to speak. He looked again at Jerry. "I guess we'd better go."

Though struggling to collect her scattered wits, Kendall nonetheless realized that he still seemed strangely reluctant to go, and suddenly she thought she knew what was bothering him. "I am acquainted with Dr. Morrissy," she said without really considering the wisdom of her words. "He is very good, you know. I'm sure no matter how bad that tooth is, he will do his best not to hurt you."

Langston had half turned away from her, but at this forthright statement, he turned quickly back, eyes snapping. Did she dare to think he was afraid of a mere dentist? The demand was as clearly written on that angry face as though he had spoken the words aloud.

"Miss Blake, if I want your advice, I'll ask for it! This stupid tooth is an inconvenience, nothing more. And why the devil I should be justifying myself to you," he added bitterly, "I'm damned if I know. Let's go, Jerry." After the brief, electrifying moment they had just shared, it was as though he had slapped her. But before she could react in any way at all, he and Jerry were gone.

"Not the most tactful thing you might have said," Sylvia Hutton said sweetly when their footsteps had faded in the distance. "But you hit him right where he lives, you know. The only reason we finally got him to agree to Dr. Morrissy is that the tooth is hurting him more than the drill will. He absolutely hates pain."

"Everyone hates pain," Kendall said, feeling a need to maintain some sort of innocuous conversation, especially now that she was alone again with Miss Hutton. "They've developed quite a few methods to make things wonderfully painless now, however." She was hardly an authority on the subject of dentists, since her own teeth were nearly perfect. For some reason, cavities simply didn't develop. She had had two when she was thirteen—none before or since. It was a family trait on her father's side. He had died two years before with only a single silver filling in his head. And his younger sister—Kendall's Aunt Alice, over in Salinas—was fifty-four and still didn't have a single one.

Sylvia Hutton had recovered from her short lapse into normal human behavior. "Will you come this way," she said stiffly. "We may as well begin with the ground floor."

Kendall followed cheerfully enough. Now that Langston had gone, she had regained her usual poise and was looking forward to seeing the rest of the house. The first thing she learned was that, although he had purchased the Sandcastle some years before, it was only within the past few months that Langston had decided to take up permanent residence there.

"He sold the brownstone in New York," Sylvia explained, "and took an apartment. He'll keep that, since he will still have a lot of business to attend to on the east coast. But slowly and steadily, he's been moving the headquarters to his office here."

"That's that flattish stone Goliath over on the Monterey Highway, isn't it?"

"Yes. He's got just as many interests now in the Orient as he has in Europe and South America, so the west coast office is really more convenient for him. And now that property taxes here have dropped . . ." Her voice trailed off, and she gave an expressive shrug.

"But why here? Why not San Francisco or L.A.?"

"Los Angeles," pronounced Miss Hutton in quelling accents, "is hardly a suitable place for anyone to live—if, indeed, living is even possible with all that dreadful smog. And San Francisco did not appeal to Steve. He prefers the pace here. He likes to play golf, too, if he gets the opportunity—not that he will much—but this is certainly the place for it."

"It certainly is," Kendall agreed, looking around with interest at the room they had just entered. It was a corner room, complete with a little round side chamber in one of the castle's turrets. She liked it, although at the moment it had little to offer aside from its interesting shape. "Tell me more about Mr. Langston's likes and dislikes," she said absently as she moved to inspect the view from the rounded chamber.

"I can scarcely see how that will interest you," said Miss Hutton frostily.

"Oh, but it does," Kendall returned evenly. "We must know what sorts of things he likes in order to provide the proper setting for him. It would never do to give him a formal setting if he prefers casual, or a classic one if he prefers a sporting look. Surely, you see my point."

"Indeed, but I already know Mr. Langston intimately, and

I assure you I do know precisely what is wanted here, Miss Blake. We'll go upstairs now, if you please."

Resigned, if only for the moment, Kendall followed in Miss Hutton's wake. It was a beautiful house. She quickly discovered that the castle illusion had not been carried to excess. Nearly the whole back side of the house was composed of windows, giving a constant, glorious view of forest and sea; and, since the Sandcastle had been carefully situated so that no other house obscured the view, there was also a sense of isolation. It was a restful house, calm and comfortable. If she had her own way in the matter, she would keep it so. Let it take its vitality from the elements. Let it reflect the natural glories on its doorstep. It occurred to her that a restful atmosphere might prove beneficial to the Sandcastle's owner, too. Not that it would—if what she had seen so far was typical behavior—be a reflection of his personality. But in this case, no doubt, it would be a good idea to provide a buffer of sorts. Otherwise, what with the natural power of Mother Nature outside and the fiery Mr. Langston inside, any excitement of decor would likely prove to be a final straw and bring the Sandcastle crashing down around all their ears. The thought made her smile.

They reentered the huge living room, and Kendall's reveries were broken when Miss Hutton asked if she wanted more coffee.

"No, thank you. I really must be going soon." But she took her seat on one of the small chintz sofas set perpendicularly to the huge window wall. "I take it that Mr. Langston wants the entire house done."

"From what he said today, he wants whatever range of services you deem most suitable. You will clear everything through me, of course." She poured herself a cup of coffee but remained standing while she sipped. "I understand that you wish to have at least one more appointment with Steve. His schedule is overflowing at the moment, but I'm sure I can fit something in either next week or the week after."

Kendall caught herself just short of gritting her teeth. "It really is extremely important that I finish the color analysis, Miss Hutton. We can do very little without it."

"Isn't that rather silly? You said you knew what category he fits into, so I should think you ought to be able to work from there. Didn't you mention a palette? Let me see it. I'm sure I can help."

It was true that Kendall had enough information to begin working, but she found herself oddly reluctant to acknowledge the fact. She wanted the job to be perfect, to get the background setting for Stephen Langston absolutely right. There was little she could say to justify her position to Miss Hutton, however, so after only a brief hesitation, she removed the portfolio of summer color swatches from her satchel and laid it upon the coffee table.

Setting her cup aside, Miss Hutton picked up the portfolio and flipped swatch after swatch, but before she was halfway through, she was frowning. Finally, she snapped the folder shut and handed it back to Kendall. "Those colors simply won't do at all, Miss Blake. I can tell you that right now. They are far too cold. Even those pinks have a chilly feel to them. They're depressing. Anyone can see that this whole place is already ice-bitten. It needs warmth, vitality, not an additional touch of frost."

"Please, Miss Hutton, let me explain."

"Nonsense. What else have you got?" Without so much as asking permission, she dove her hand into Kendall's leather satchel and came up with the other three portfolios. Flipping quickly through them, she fairly pounced on the one labeled Autumn. Kendall's eyes gleamed with resigned amusement. "Here we are. Now, this is exactly the sort of thing I mean. Steve said he wants to keep to the basics—earth tones, you know. And here they are. He doesn't like to *wear* brown, of course, but brown carpeting or a brown chair would be an entirely different matter. And these golden tans and mossy greens will be splendid with accessories in yellow or orange. Perhaps even a touch of this lovely flame red. These will be perfect, Miss Blake. Exactly right."

"Those colors are not suitable for Mr. Langston," Kendall said carefully, torn between amusement and exasperation. "He would be overwhelmed by them, believe me."

"Nonsense!" exclaimed Miss Hutton tartly. "Many of these colors are the very ones I chose for my own apartment, and Steve adores it. In fact, that was the main reason he pleaded with me to take on this project. I can assure you that decorating houses is not normally one of my duties."

Kendall felt an unexpected twinge of something perilously akin to jealousy at the thought that Langston had been in Miss Hutton's apartment, but that sensation was quickly replaced by an uncanny illusion of Meg standing at her shoulder, warning her to be tactful, flattering if necessary, to do what she could to calm Miss Hutton. It took an effort, nevertheless.

"I'm sure Mr. Langston *would* have liked your apartment if these were the colors you selected," she said quietly. "They are your best colors, Miss Hutton, so he would be seeing you at your most attractive. I've no doubt that you have excellent taste in furnishings, too, but I assure you that Mr. Langston would soon be quite worn out by an entire house decorated in such warm and vibrant colors."

"He is a warm and vibrant man," Miss Hutton replied flatly. "The colors of his home should reflect that."

"On the contrary," Kendall disagreed. "The colors of his home should complement his own coloring. He would only clash with your oranges and yellows. Mind you, I'm not saying we can't use them for accessories here and there if you insist upon it. But the touches must be subtle ones, unless—" She broke off as a thought occurred to her, striking like an unpleasant electrical shock. "Unless you will also be living here. If that is a possibility, it is certainly one we should be aware of."

Sylvia Hutton's look was nearly glacial. "That factor is completely irrelevant, Miss Blake. Suffice it to say that I shall have very little trouble convincing Steve Langston that my color choices are the correct ones."

"I see." Aware of a ridiculous sense of depression, Kendall picked up her things from the table and got to her feet. "My partner will want to see the house tomorrow. She will need to sketch floor plans and so forth. Is it necessary to set a time now for her arrival?"

"Not at all. She can come when she likes. I'll leave word at the City Gate. If she comes by any other route, just tell her to call the house if they won't let her pass."

Kendall nodded. At least, she thought, it sounded as though the woman had no intention of hovering over them every step of the way. But she was going to cause major problems if the color business wasn't settled quickly. Slipping her purse over her shoulder, Kendall picked up her satchel and followed Miss Hutton to the door.

On the doorstep, the other woman spoke crisply. "I'll expect to hear from you as soon as you have worked up an idea or two. But remember, not a step without my approval. You can reach me at the main office usually, but if I'm out, just leave a message with my secretary. Mr. Langston will not want to be bothered with details."

And that puts you firmly in your place, my girl, Kendall told herself as she crunched her way across the gravel drive to the little Camaro. Tossing her satchel into the backseat, she wondered briefly why she was not more annoyed than she was. But when it occurred to her that she was still recovering from Langston's shattering effect upon her psyche, she suppressed both thoughts sternly, slipped on her sunglasses, and guided the Camaro through the opening gates and onto the main road. A mile or so further on, she turned up the little lane she had passed earlier and soon pulled into the open driveway beside Hilda Quick's little house.

As she stepped from the car, she pushed her sunglasses high onto her head and gazed appreciatively at the single-story, rough-timber-and-glass structure half hidden by majestic pines and crooked cypress trees. Ivy spread itself across the low hill in front of the house, kept within bounds of sorts by a pattern of railway ties. More ties, terracing spongy green dichondra, supplied the steps from driveway to the redwood deck surrounding the house. Kendall closed the car door and began to climb the steps, but the front door opened before she reached it, and Hilda Quick hurried forward, arms spread wide, to meet her.

"The kettle's on!" she said happily. "Come in, child, come in!"

Hilda was well past fifty but still striking enough to cause pangs of envy in women twenty years her junior. Tall and slender, she looked as Vogue-cover elegant in Levis as in an evening gown. At the moment, she was wearing royal blue slacks with a snow white Irish-wool sweater. Her sparkling eyes were nearly the same color as the slacks, and her dark brown hair showed not the slightest touch of gray. Kendall didn't know whether the latter detail was due to the expertise of Hilda's hairdresser or to the hair's own knowledge that any hint of graying would be ruthlessly dealt with. But natural or not, its present style was one Kendall particularly liked. Parted in the middle and winged over the temples, the main bulk of hair was confined against the back of Hilda's neck in an intricately woven yet soft-looking bun. Kendall never had been able to understand its secret, though she had watched Hilda accomplish the same look scores of times. She just seemed to grab the long hank of back hair, and twist it into a sort of loose knot. Ten seconds, and presto—exquisite elegance.

Kendall walked straight into Aunt Hilda's arms and returned the hug with interest. Meg's whole family was demonstrative, which was another thing about them that had taken some getting used to. Kendall's family, in her older brother George's words, were more civilized than to go about pawing and smooching. But George was safely in Connecticut with a prim wife and two outwardly well-behaved children; her father was dead; and her mother was somewhere in Europe on one of her prolonged peregrinations. Consequently, Kendall could accept the love and friendship of the Potter tribe without a single discomfiting thought as to whether such behavior was "done" or not.

"How are you, Aunt Hilda?" she asked now. "You look absolutely smashing in that getup."

"My colors, aren't they? Yours too, for that matter. Must be why we have such a mutual admiration society going. But come on in, and tell me what you think of that Langston boy."

Kendall's eyes twinkled as she tried to imagine what Langston would think of such a label, but her usually fertile imagination failed her. She followed Hilda through the pristine entry hall into the spacious living room. Everything, everywhere, was white, and Kendall loved it. Meg had been doubtful at first, but Kendall had given Aunt Hilda's notions her firm support, and this lovely, serene setting was the result. At the moment, there were various emerald green pillows scattered about, and the dining table in the little alcove near the kitchen had been laid with a crisp white, lace-trimmed cloth and emerald green place mats. But except for the books in the floor-to-ceiling cases flanking the fireplace, and the cheerful little fire blazing merrily away behind the built-in glass fire screen, there was no other color but the greens and browns of the forest beyond the huge windows. Hilda changed the pillows and place mats regularly, thus, she said, effectively changing the whole tempo of her life-style.

Not just the living room but the entire house had been done in white. Any other color appeared only in touches that could be easily changed. Nevertheless, even at its starkest, and despite Meg's oft-voiced fears, the house never looked antiseptic or chilly, but always elegant, cozy, and serene. It suited its owner perfectly.

"Sit, sit!" Hilda chuckled when Kendall started to follow her into the tiny kitchen. "You'll only get in the way. It's a one-woman kitchen, as you know perfectly well. Go talk to Purr-See, but don't tell him a thing you won't want to repeat."

Kendall smiled and turned back toward the fireplace, noting for the first time the huge white, long-haired cat perched upon the overstuffed arm of the sofa, his dainty forepaws tucked neatly under his fluffy chest. Unblinking aquamarine eyes surveyed her from under haughty brows, and one pink-tipped ear twitched in dignified acknowledgment of her presence.

"Good afternoon, Purr-See," she said quietly, careful to accent the second syllable. He did not approve of people who mistakenly called him Percy. She reached out to caress him gently between the ears, and he expressed his welcome by pushing his head quite firmly against her fingers. His purr was the only thing about him that was not refined. Hilda had often described the sound as one resembling a garbage disposal gone haywire. She entered now, carrying a tray, and Kendall turned toward her and took a seat on the sofa, ignoring the small rasp of protest from the cat.

The tray soon reposed between them on a glass-topped coffee table, and she took her first appreciative sip of the spicy, sweet tea.

"Well, what did you think of him?" Hilda asked bluntly. Kendall blinked at her.

"Who? Oh, Stephen Langston?" She reached for a cigarette and lit it, her eyes twinkling in response to Hilda's undisguised impatience. "Well, if you must have it, Aunt Hilda, I thought he was overbearing, rude, temperamental, and childishly volatile." Warming to her subject, she went on more tartly. "He's one of the biggest men I've ever seen, and he began our acquaintance by nearly knocking me flat through not watching where he was going. Then he puffed off about the view from his living room like a kid bragging about a new toy. His assistant, Miss Hutton, is a tale unto herself—a veritable witch—but she treats him like some species of god. I thought at first that she considered him her personal property, but he behaves as if he thinks she is there simply to pass on his orders to others and to pour his coffee for him. I'm sure her attitude is merely an attempt to show everyone, including his highness, that she is more important than that, and that even being in charge of redecorating his house is a task well beneath her capabilities."

A look from Miss Quick informed Kendall that that lady had heard quite enough about Miss Hutton, thank you, and would appreciate it if she would get back to the main attraction.

Kendall's eyes reflected her amusement. "All right, enough about Miss Hutton, but his attitude toward me was nearly as patronizing. He's also a male chauvinist about color —thinks brown is for hicks and pink is for sissies. And he's afraid of his dentist, but he doesn't like anyone else to guess it. In the space of half an hour he threw two near temper tantrums that made me long to smack him. And . . . and . . ." Suddenly Kendall seemed to have run out of steam. With a sigh, she cast a rueful sidelong glance at Hilda, and her voice dropped to a reluctant mutter. "And he's got the twinkliest eyes you've ever seen, a voice like mellifluous velvet, and a grin that would charm the devil out of hell."

Hilda chuckled with wicked delight. "Do go on, child. This sounds promising. Very promising indeed!"

CHAPTER 3

During the short drive back to Carmel, Kendall thought over her conversation with Hilda, who had insisted upon hearing every detail of her visit to the Sandcastle. Talking about it had helped to put things into perspective, and she realized that her first priority must be to clear up the color matter as soon as possible. Neither she nor Meg would be able to accomplish much if they had to battle out each detail with Sylvia Hutton.

Hilda had listened to her with rapt interest, but she had offered no advice. It was one of the things Kendall liked best about the older woman. All she had said once the whole story had been laid before her was, "Well, my dear, one way or another, you will have to make a decision and stick to it."

But what decision, Kendall wondered as she nosed the car up Second Avenue. She could hardly tell Sylvia Hutton to mind her own business if Langston had put her in charge of the project. She adjusted her sunglasses and slowed for a car that insisted upon possession of the few inches of space between the Camaro and the blue Plymouth ahead of it. This was not the time to grapple with knotty mental problems. She would have to discuss things with Meg before making any decisions anyway. She stopped at the post office to pick up their mail, then drove to the studio.

Pert, freckle-faced Sally Hunt, their part-time office assistant, was on the phone and scribbling notes when Kendall walked in. In response to an inquiring eyebrow, she jerked her head toward the workroom, and Kendall went on through to find Meg sitting on the floor amidst a multicolored pile of velvets and laces. She looked up, then waved at the mess around her, laughing. "Hi. I'm trying to decide what goes with what for those pillows Mrs. Ashton wants. Oh, and before I forget, you're supposed to call Stephen Langston. His office number's on your desk." Her eyes twinkled.

Kendall had come to a full stop in the doorway, and she gazed searchingly at her partner, momentarily forgetting the small handful of letters she carried. "Did he say what it was about? Or—I suppose it was actually his secretary on the phone."

"Nope. The great man himself," Meg replied with a grin. "But he didn't say. I called Aunt Hilda's, figuring you'd stop there on your way home, but you'd already gone. Aunt Hilda says Langston knocked you for a loop, and from that frozen look on your face, I'd say she has a point. Are those letters for me?"

"Aunt Hilda's an incurable romantic," Kendall murmured vaguely as she obediently handed Meg her mail. "I wonder what he wants."

"One way to find out," Meg retorted. She flipped through the letters, but wrinkled her small nose when she found nothing of particular interest. Then she grinned at Kendall. "What's he like?"

After watering down the description she had given Hilda, Kendall added, "But he won't be a problem. You should be asking me about Miss Hutton instead."

"His executive assistant?"

"Grand title, isn't it? I wonder how the job description reads." She leaned against the doorjamb.

"You think she's like those Washington secretaries? All looks, and no typing or dictation?"

Kendall gave the idea some serious thought. "She wouldn't like being dictated to by anyone, if you don't mind the play on words. I think she would go to bed with the boss if he so much as crooked his little finger, and if she thought it would be good for her career, but I didn't get the impression from him that things are like that. She did seem a tad possessive though."

"Staking out her territory?"

Kendall frowned. "I'm not sure. She's ambitious. I really think her career comes first, but that ambition might conceivably include a wedding ring from the boss. I just don't know. I'm pretty sure he doesn't know about it if she *is* interested in marriage. But the important thing as far as we're concerned is that he's put her in charge, and she means to have the house done her way. The problem is that she's an autumn. Langston is summer."

"Oh dear," Meg said, eyes wide. She required no further explanation. They had run into the problem before. "That could mean real trouble. I do wish that when people hire us to do a thing, they would let us get on with it our way. Perhaps I could explain things to Miss Hutton."

Kendall shook her head. She had no doubt that Meg would handle Sylvia Hutton far better than she could, simply because Meg was a natural-born diplomat, which God knew she was not. But Sylvia Hutton was clearly as stubborn as they came. While she was trying to explain that little fact, another thing Meg had said began to buzz around in her head. They had been hired to do a job, and then the very person who hired them had made it nearly impossible for them to get on with it.

The whole time they had been talking, Meg had continued to sort her velvets. Now, she waved her hand over the mess. "This is going to take a while. Want to help?"

Kendall straightened, giving the pile of laces and velvets a cursory glance. Mrs. Ashton was a fluffy, pink-cheeked, blue-eyed widow who lived alone in a gingerbreaded Victorian wedding-cake house in Pacific Grove. She had come to them for help in choosing new colors for her parlor, and Meg had agreed to make some throw pillows for her. The two of them could certainly finish the job more quickly than Meg could do it alone, but Kendall's mind refused to concentrate on fluff at the moment. "I'll help you later," she said finally, drawing a deep breath. "When I get back."

"Back? Where are you going?"

"To Langston Industries." Kendall's reply was decisive. She pulled her compact from her purse to check her makeup.

"But he only said to call!"

"I know. But I'll handle this better in person than I would over the phone."

"Handle what?" Meg asked suspiciously. "Kendall, what are you going to do?"

The gray green eyes twinkled back at her. "I'm going directly to the source of our problem, my dear. I'm going to set Mr. Langston straight about how Blake and Potter do business."

"Oh, Kendall, no! You'll only annoy him. This is the biggest job we've ever had. What if he says he doesn't want us, after all?"

"He won't," Kendall assured her, wishing she believed that herself, "but I promise you we wouldn't want the job if it meant we'd have to work under Miss Hutton's thumb."

"Yes, we would!" Meg cried, coming to her knees in agitation and sending velvets and laces scattering. "Kendall Blake, don't you dare louse this up, or I'll never speak to you again. I mean it. I can handle your Miss Hutton. You know I can!"

"Maybe you could at that," Kendall agreed. "But Langston hired us because we're supposed to know our business. And we do know it. We're good. He ought to trust us to do the thing properly and without putting that obstructive feline in our way."

"My," Meg said slowly, subsiding back into her velvets, "you didn't like her, did you?"

"No."

Meg said nothing more except to mention that Jack Susmann had also called to remind Kendall that he would pick her up at six-fifteen to take her to dinner. Kendall, her mind on the upcoming interview with Langston, merely nodded vaguely.

Soon afterward, she found herself back in the little

Camaro, and fifteen minutes later, she had turned onto
Route 68, the Monterey-Salinas Highway, a two-lane road
that wound its way through beautiful, rolling golden hills
dotted with dark green, sprawling oak trees. It was just about
her favorite place to drive in the whole country. There had
been times when she had been far from home that she had
laid back, closed her eyes, and driven an imaginary car from
Monterey to Salinas and back again. She knew every hill,
every curve, every fence, every tree.

Twilight was rapidly approaching as she passed the Airport
Road and Robert Talbot's, the famous tiemaker who had
started with a little tie shop at the bottom of Ocean Avenue
and finally achieved the sort of success that warranted building this huge place.

A mile or so past Talbot's, she found the turn she was
looking for and soon pulled into a parking space in front of
the low stone building that housed the main offices of Langston Industries. It suited its location, blending into the hillside as though it had always been there. Beds of juniper and
poppies surrounded the building, giving it a cheerful air. But
Kendall noticed immediately that, aside from the front
doors, there didn't seem to be any glass at all. No windows!
How very peculiar, she thought. Not at all what one might
have expected for the sort of man Langston had seemed to
be. Not after he had made such a point of the magnificent
view from the Sandcastle. The view here would be different,
of course, but no less rewarding with all the golden hills and
beautiful oak trees.

There was a uniformed security guard at a desk just inside
the front door. He even carried a pistol. That fact, coupled
with the lack of windows, made her suspect briefly that something in the building might require tight security, but when
she said she had come to see Mr. Langston, the guard let her
pass without difficulty, even giving her the directions she
requested in a courteous, smiling manner. His behavior
scarcely suggested that there were deep, dark secrets to be

guarded, but Kendall found her curiosity whetted, nonetheless.

Langston's office was quite easy to find, being at the end of a wide corridor facing the entrance. Huge double doors opened at a mere touch, and Kendall found herself in a spacious, comfortable reception room. A pretty, red-headed receptionist glanced up from a chrome-and-glass desk and smiled cordially.

"May I help you?"

"Yes, please. I'm here to see Mr. Langston."

"Of course. Do you have an appointment?"

"No, but—"

"Oh." A shadow crossed the exquisitely made-up features. "Then I'm afraid Mr. Langston couldn't possibly see you now," she said regretfully. "His schedule is very tight."

"Mr. Langston will see me," Kendall replied with cool assurance. "All you need do, Miss . . ."—her gaze flicked over the unpretentious nameplate placed near the front edge of the desk—". . . Miss Welch, is to ring through to him and tell him that Miss Kendall Blake, of Blake and Potter, is returning his call."

Miss Welch's almond-shaped brown eyes narrowed in a look that was as appreciative as it was searching, but Kendall returned it with a steady one of her own. Miss Welch capitulated.

"Very well," she agreed doubtfully, reaching for one of several buttons on her callbox. The familiar, deep voice responded immediately, conjuring a vision in Kendall's mind of the tall, broad-shouldered man as she had last seen him.

"What is it, Sandra?"

"Miss Kendall Blake, sir," replied the receptionist, watching Kendall.

"Put her through," came the order.

"She's here, sir."

"Here! What the devil's she doing here?"

"She says," returned Miss Welch carefully, the amusement

in her eyes never reaching her voice, "that she is returning your call, Mr. Langston."

"She's a downright impudent female, if you ask me," he retorted with a chuckle. "Well, don't keep her waiting, Sandra. Show the lady in."

Miss Welch smiled and stood up, moving toward another set of double doors behind her desk and to the left. "Your trick, I believe, Miss Blake."

Kendall smiled back and stepped lightly after her, repressing a sudden urge to smooth her skirt or straighten her jacket. Then she realized that her sunglasses were still perched atop her head where she had shoved them when it grew too dark to see through them. She snatched them off, slipping them into her jacket pocket just before Miss Welch pulled open the doors.

"Miss Blake, sir."

"Thank you, Sandra. Hold my calls." With a crooked little smile Stephen Langston got to his feet and moved around his paper-ridden desk, holding out a welcoming hand as Kendall stepped toward him. There was the same sense of cluttered comfort here, she noted, as in the study at the Sandcastle. It was a sort of organized chaos, giving any chance visitor a feeling of energy at work. "Good afternoon again, Miss Blake," Langston said, taking her hand in that firm, warm grasp. But this meeting was very important, and she had steeled herself to retain her dignity. She returned the handshake briefly, then firmly withdrew her hand. He smiled more broadly, as though something in her attitude amused him. "This is more than I'd expected, you know. Sit down."

"Well, I didn't know why you called, of course," Kendall replied, keeping her expression serious but obeying him by perching on the edge of a small sofa near the desk. "However, I wanted to speak to you about something rather important, anyway, and I do that sort of thing better in person."

"I called you because I owed you an apology," Langston said bluntly. "There was no excuse for my rudeness earlier. I behaved like a child, and I wanted to ask you to forgive me."

Kendall stared at him. It was the last thing she had expected him to say. "Oh dear," she breathed slowly.

"Does that mean you can't bring yourself to forgive me?"

"No, of course not. It was just—"

"Unexpected?" He grinned. "Good. I like to keep my ladies guessing. Will you have dinner with me tonight?"

Kendall felt as though the wind had been taken out of her sails. This was not at all the sort of conversation she had anticipated having with him. His ladies indeed!

"Mr. Langston," she began after a long, steadying breath, "I came here to discuss a matter of business, and I take my business very seriously." She shot him a speaking look. "And I wish you will sit down, sir. I feel as though I'm attempting to converse with the Eiffel Tower. If you insist upon standing, I'm certain to acquire a crick in my neck at the very least."

He grinned back at her, but she had struck a no doubt familiar and therefore responsive chord, for he moved obediently to the chair behind his desk and sat down. "Go ahead, Miss Blake," he said then on a more serious note. "What seems to be the problem?"

"Your Miss Hutton," Kendall replied calmly, but she braced herself for fireworks. Meg would say she ought to be more tactful, and certainly Langston seemed to be the sort best handled with kid gloves. But something about him kept her from sidestepping the main issue. And, so far at least, he hadn't exploded.

His eyes narrowed a bit, but his tone seemed only curious. "What has Sylvia done to upset you?"

"It's not what she's done exactly. It's what she plans to do. I need to know how much I am to rely upon my own instincts and experience and how much I must bow to hers. In short, Mr. Langston, are we working for you or for Miss Hutton?"

"Easy enough. You are working for me, but since I am too busy to oversee the project, Sylvia is acting in my place. She speaks for me, and when you speak to her, you will also be speaking to me."

"No," Kendall said flatly. There was a small silence.

"Would you care to elaborate on that?" he asked softly. Somehow, the gentler tone sounded far more dangerous to her than his shouting had done earlier. She swallowed carefully and forced her suddenly nervous hands to relax in her lap. Why on earth did this man affect her hitherto well-behaved emotions so strongly? At the moment there seemed to be a veritable war of butterflies in her stomach. But she would not allow either Langston or his assistant to browbeat her. She faced him squarely.

"I have no doubt that Miss Hutton is extremely competent, sir, but she cannot stand in your place as far as this particular project is concerned. It is your house, not hers. If her coloring were similar to yours, or if she were also going to live there, it might work, but it's not, and you haven't mentioned that she is, so it won't."

"You will have to have dinner with me," he said decisively.

Kendall's eyes flashed, and she fairly bristled with indignation. "Are you saying that I must dine with you before—"

"Don't say it!" he snapped abruptly. "Of course, I'm not saying anything of the sort. It's not blackmail, extortion, or anything even remotely like that. But Sandra is no doubt holding off at least five or six callers by now, and I can see that there is really a problem of some kind here. But, since I still don't perfectly understand the nature of it, I'm certainly not going to go off half-cocked on a partial explanation from you." He stood up again, adding more gently, "I've got matters to clear up here, but I've been looking for an excuse to cancel what promised to be a rather boring evening. This will do much better than anything else that might possibly have come my way. We can talk the whole thing out over a good meal. Now, what do you say?"

Kendall ignored both her thudding heart and Jack Susmann's prior claim to her company for the evening. "I should like that very much, sir," she said, "but there is one small favor I would ask of you, if you don't mind."

"Name it, but stop calling me sir."

"If you will pick me up at the studio," she returned evenly,

"I can finish that color analysis in just a few moments. You would also have a chance to meet Meg Potter."

"Done, unless it means I can't drive you home after dinner. I'm sure you're a typically modern young woman and can take excellent care of yourself, but I won't take you out wining and dining and then just drop you at your car afterward."

"No, sir, that won't be necessary. Meg's cottage is about halfway between my house and the studio, and she usually walks to work. But she's staying late tonight. She'll be glad to drive my car home, and I'll just walk over to her place in the morning, or she can pick me up."

"Good. Then I'll meet you about six-thirty, *ma'am.*"

Kendall chuckled appreciatively, reaching for the purse on the sofa beside her and therefore not noticing the expression her sudden, dazzling smile brought to Langston's face. "Your point, Mr. Langston. Six-thirty, it is." She stood and moved toward the door.

"The name is Steve, blast you!"

"Yes, sir," she shot back, eyes dancing. But before he could respond, she slipped through the door into the reception room, nodded at Miss Welch, and hurried on through the wide corridor to the front lobby. It wasn't until she reached the glass front door that she remembered the lack of windows in the place. But now that she came to think about it, she realized that there hadn't been any windows in Steve Langston's office or in the reception room either. There had been lots of shelves and a painting or two, as well as that sense of organized chaos, but she had difficulty remembering details. She only knew that she hadn't missed the presence of windows.

She hurried across the well-lit parking lot toward her car. Should she wear a businesslike suit or something sexier? She knew what Langston's preference would be, but a suit would certainly help to keep matters on a business level. She had that charcoal gray wool-gabardine, and the lemon silk blouse had just come back from the cleaners. She opened the car door and slid in, mentally chiding herself.

"Who are you trying to kid, my girl?" she whispered to the rearview mirror image staring dimly back at her. "It's the hot pink cashmere or nothing!"

She glanced at her watch. It was already past five, and Langston had said six-thirty. She had a strong notion that he was the punctual type, too, so with a wary eye peeled for the California Highway Patrol, she drove back to Carmel as fast as she dared. Avoiding the traffic on Ocean Avenue, she crossed behind the Plaza to Eighth Street and followed it to the beach front, where she turned left, that being the only direction one could turn. There were certain disadvantages to living on the only one-way street in Carmel, but Kendall could remember the grim days of two-way traffic on Scenic Road and was one of the many who had applauded the change. Moments later, she parked the Camaro in the carport that had been dug out of the hillside just below the medium-sized, white-trimmed gray house she called home.

As she climbed the flagstone steps to the gate, she could hear the murmur and splash of waves behind and below her. The eight-foot gate creaked when she pushed it open, sounding almost as raucous as the gulls that screeched overhead during the day, and she remembered that she had meant to oil it. She always remembered when she opened or closed it, never when she might have the time to attend to it. Jack had said he would see to it, but he always forgot, too. She had also forgotten, again, to leave the porch light on. That was annoying but no longer as frightening as it had been when she first moved into the beachfront house.

She didn't have time to worry about light or gate now anyway, with less than an hour to get ready, but thinking of Jack made her remember that she had to call him to break their date. Kendall rarely broke dates. A commitment was a commitment. But this was business, she told herself firmly. That made it a different matter altogether. Jack would just have to understand. Nevertheless, there were twinges of guilt as she hurried down the dark flagstone walkway alongside the house and let herself in. Flipping the switch, she felt the familiar sense of satisfaction as the lights came on, casting their warm indirect glow over the comfortable living room.

This house had been one of the first she and Meg had done. It belonged to one of the "prominent" clients Meg had mentioned earlier in the day. Kendall thought of Peter and Loretta Kingsley with fondness. They were close friends of her family's, but Peter's business kept them on the go most of the time. They were presently living in London and had offered Kendall the use of their Carmel house as soon as they'd discovered her intention to move back to the Peninsula. She had accepted gratefully but had also insisted that she must be allowed to pay rent. Over the phone, Peter Kingsley had laughingly agreed to a very modest sum and then had nearly overwhelmed her by commanding that, since she would be right on the spot, she might as well redo the place and send the bills to him.

"But I can't do that!" she had protested.

"Nonsense," Peter chuckled. "The house has needed it for years. And don't tell me you girls can't use the work, because you're just getting your feet wet now, and I know better. Just do the thing, and send me the bill."

And that had been that. The house was small—a spacious living room, two bedrooms, a tiny kitchen-dinette, and a bath and a half. But there was also a guest cottage in back—just a bedroom and bath, but Kendall had decided that if the Kingsleys wanted to visit Carmel, she could move back there for the duration of their stay.

She and Meg had loved redoing the house. Luckily, both Kingsleys had winter coloring like Kendall, so she could use her own best colors without the slightest qualm. It was convenient, to say the least, but it was not much of a coincidence, since quite half of the world's population fell into the winter category. Nevertheless, it meant Kendall could give free rein to her own taste and Meg's talent.

They had chosen taupe as the basic color for the wide living room, covering the floor with plush wool carpeting that extended down the hall and into the two bedrooms. For the living-room walls, Meg had selected a burlap-textured wallpaper in the same shade. The classic sofa and matching chair had been recovered in narrow burgundy stripes, and Peter Kingsley's huge wine red leather chair had seemed right at home. Touches of navy and silver and a selection of wharf scenes for the walls had finished the room, giving it a sense of simple elegance and comfort.

Kendall passed quickly through it now and hurried down the hall to the larger of the two bedrooms. Here, the walls were covered with pinstripes of dark gray-green that nearly matched her eyes. The solid-colored velvet drapes were the same shade, and the spread on the king-size bed was of patchwork velvet, its pattern carried out in various shades of green and gray with an intricate design of bright red stitching. Meg had found the quilted spread at a craft fair in Marina and had been so sure of its suitability for the room that she had promptly purchased it without so much as a telephone consultation.

Quickly, Kendall pulled off her clothes, automatically hanging up her skirt and jacket, and dropping blouse and underwear in the gray wicker hamper near the bathroom door. She was by nature a very tidy person, and the house was immaculate. Cleaning relaxed her, and she often cleaned house just to shed her tensions. She reached in and turned on the shower before twisting her hair up into the bright yellow shower cap. She had shampooed her hair only the day before, which was a very good thing, she thought, since she certainly didn't have time to do so now. She put a tentative hand under the shower. Perfect. A moment later, lathering soap over herself, she remembered she hadn't called Jack.

"Damn," she muttered aloud, scrubbing faster. He was not going to be at all understanding if she let him drive over from Monterey only to be told at the door that he would be eating alone tonight. She gave a final scrub to her face, rinsed herself off, and leaned out of the shower to grab the huge yellow bath sheet hanging on a ring in a pewter lion's mouth on the wall next to the shower.

Wrapping herself in its fleecy warmth, she hurried over to the phone on the night table, sitting on the bed and pushing the familiar numbers with practiced speed. By the fourth ring, she was sure he had already gone, but just as she was about to return the phone to its cradle, the ringing stopped abruptly, and a slightly out-of-breath masculine voice answered.

"Oh, Jack," Kendall said quickly, "I'm glad I caught you."

"Barely," he admitted. "Had to unlock the door to get back in. I'm just on my way, babe."

"I can't go, Jack," she said more brusquely than she'd intended. She hated to be called babe. "I've got to meet a client."

"A client? Isn't this rather sudden?"

"Yes, of course it is. But we've got a problem with a new job, and the only time he can spare is tonight. It's important, Jack. You know I wouldn't break our date if it weren't."

"I know." But there was a doubtful note in his voice. Kendall glanced anxiously at the little clock next to the phone. Ten to six. "Who is this guy anyway, babe?"

She wanted to tell him it was none of his business, but Jack was a good friend even if she didn't plan to spend her life with him. "It's Stephen Langston."

"You don't say!" he exclaimed. "That's definitely big time stuff, babe, but you'd better wear a suit of armor. That guy's got quite a reputation with the ladies."

"I wouldn't know about that," Kendall replied stiffly, remembering Langston's own comment about his *ladies*, "but I've got to go now. I'm not nearly ready."

"Well, I don't think I like the idea of you going out alone with a guy like him. If it's business, how come Meg isn't going, too?"

"Don't start, Jack. I haven't got time to argue with you. Believe me, I'm a big girl, and I can take care of myself. I'm sorry about our date, but I really do have to go now."

He let her ring off, but she knew from the tone of his voice that he was annoyed. There would probably be a scene the next time they met, but it was nothing to worry about now. She had to get dressed.

She put on fresh underwear and her slip, and then sat down to do her makeup. Ten minutes later, she slipped the hot pink cashmere dress off the hanger and over her head. Any lingering doubts about the suitability of wearing it had evaporated. She would prove to Jack—and to Langston, for that matter—that she was professional enough to handle even an established flirt no matter what she wore.

As the caressingly soft folds slipped smoothly into place, emphasizing the sexy curves of her breasts and hips, Kendall winked at her reflection in the full-length mirror. "Hardly what one would call a suit of armor," she chuckled.

CHAPTER 4

When Kendall entered the studio, Meg was at the sewing machine. She looked up. "My, don't you look nice! Is Jack picking you up here?" She glanced at her watch. "He's late."

"Not exactly," Kendall replied, her eyes twinkling as she slipped off her gray wool fur-trimmed coat and laid it across the back of a chair. "I'm not going with Jack."

"Not—" Meg's mouth dropped open, and she stared at Kendall suspiciously. "Just what happened out at Langston Industries?"

Kendall chuckled. "Mr. Langston needs more information about our problem, and he didn't have time to talk about it right then, so he is taking me out to dinner. Strictly business, Miss Potter."

Meg let her eyes travel pointedly from the tip of Kendall's shining hair to the toes of her patent-leather slings. "Business, my eye," she said wisely. "That is hardly the traditional business-woman's garb, my dear."

"I know," Kendall admitted. "Jack said I ought to wear a suit of armor. He said Langston's got quite a reputation."

"Well, since I don't travel in those elevated circles, I wouldn't know about that, but if he can keep his hands off you when you look like that, he's got admirable willpower. You told Jack you were going out with him?"

"Well, of course I did. I could hardly break our date without an explanation."

Meg shook her head. "I wish you hadn't. Jack can be so difficult. Why all your men have to be the jealous types, I certainly don't know. But Jack is even worse than most. This business with Mr. Langston will really wind his clock, and you know it."

Kendall did know it, but there was no further time to discuss the matter, for the front door opened at that moment, and she turned to see Langston's huge form filling the doorway. The very sight of him was enough to stir the coals deep within her, and it was more difficult than ever to maintain her cool reserve.

"Hi," he said, shutting the door behind himself. "You look fantastic."

"Thank you," Kendall replied, adding quickly, "come in and meet Meg. Meg, this is Stephen Langston."

Meg got hastily to her feet as Langston entered the workroom. "How do you do, Mr. Langston. We're really looking forward to working at the Sandcastle." She held out her hand and grinned up at Langston when he stepped forward to grasp it between his own.

Kendall watched in silent appreciation as the two of them chatted amiably together. Both were so outgoing and friendly that they already looked as though they had known each other for a long time. She could never be that relaxed when she met new people. There was always a sort of distance first, and it generally took her a long time before she could feel completely comfortable with another person. Attracted as she was to Langston, she was still certain that it would be some time before she would let down her guard with him. But, on the other hand, once someone new had been added to her small circle of friends, he or she had a tendency to stay there. Meg always had at least thirty-nine best friends at any given moment, but they seemed to come and go, disappearing from her life as easily and uncomplicatedly as they entered it. Kendall envied her her ability to make friends quickly, but she found it hard to understand how Meg could let a friendship simply melt away. Meg rarely wrote letters and made no effort at all to maintain friendships made at school. Kendall, on the other hand, though she had few close friends, made it a point to maintain and cultivate those relationships.

"How do you want to do this?" Langston asked, and Kendall looked at him blankly. She had been so deep in her own thoughts that for a moment she couldn't think what he meant. Then she realized that she had promised to finish his color analysis.

"Sit in that chair over there," she commanded, regaining control of herself and pointing to a lone chair in front of a white drape. "Meg, you be our audience. Get him settled while I get my gear."

Meg escorted Langston to the chair, then switched on a bank of combined fluorescent and incandescent lights. "Artificial daylight, Steve. Our own little piece of the sun. Tell me when you can see yourself properly in the mirror. We want to avoid shadows." She tilted the large mirror on the table in front of Langston until he nodded that it was correctly placed. Then she drew up a chair of her own so that she could watch the proceedings. Kendall smiled to herself when she heard the other girl call Langston by his nickname. Old friends already, she thought with a touch of envy. Then, giving herself a mental shake, she removed the summer palette from her satchel and opened the ring that bound the swatches together.

The analysis took about a quarter of an hour, and it only took that long because Meg managed to convince Langston to let Kendall try the various shades of pink and lavender. They all agreed that his best colors were the grays and blues in the palette, but Meg pointed out that they needed all the information they could get if they were to select colors for the house properly.

"You've got to understand, Steve," she said, grinning at him, "that we aren't necessarily trying to get you to *wear* all these colors. But we do need to know if any of them would make you look like a sick little frog in your own house."

Langston laughed. "All right, Meg. But, mind you, no pink

sofas. I'd heave them right out the nearest window into the sea."

"Don't worry," Kendall said serenely. "Meg won't do anything you won't like. The Sandcastle will be absolutely perfect when she finishes with it."

"That I don't doubt," Langston replied. "Are we finished now? I'm starving." Kendall nodded and accepted Meg's offer to clear up the mess they had made. Langston helped her with her coat, and his nearness stirred the coals again. If people really did possess auras, it was as though his made hers tingle, she thought absurdly. They went outside into the crisp, clear evening.

"My car's up the street a ways," he said quietly. "Parking seems to be at a premium around here tonight."

"Always is, but that's all right," Kendall replied. "I like to walk." She made no move to resist when he took her hand and placed it in the crook of his arm. The street was poorly lit like most of Carmel's streets, and she felt more secure with her arm in his. Besides, she told herself fiercely, she needed the practice if she was ever to learn to cope with the dizzying effect his touch had upon her. She had been behaving like a starry-eyed schoolgirl, and that would never do. She could do better. Moonlight glinted on the sleek little blue and silver Datsun 280Z as Langston drew out his keys to unlock the passenger door. He watched appreciatively when she sat down with her usual graceful ease and swung her legs in daintily.

"Very neat," he commented. "Most women look awkward to say the least when they climb into a low-slung car. You make it look easy."

"It is easy," she replied in her husky voice. "We learned how to do it properly at school. Also how to get into the backseat of a car without looking like a camel."

He chuckled, shut the door, and strode around to the other door. In retaliation, Kendall watched pointedly to see how he would fold himself into such a small car, but he had no trouble. He grinned at her. "See, I can do it, too. I'll admit though that one of the reasons I bought this car was that it gives me the headroom I need. What school did you go to?"

"Mills College."

He gave a low whistle. "But that's one of the finest women's colleges on the west coast," he said, shooting an accusing look at her as he switched on the engine. "You can't mean you actually had classes in how to get in and out of cars!"

"Well, there were other classes, too, of course," Kendall said wryly. "But that was my favorite."

"I know what you mean," he laughed. "I went to MIT, and we had some peculiar things to get through there, too." He eased the Datsun out of its space and drove up to the first intersection, where he deftly made a U-turn and headed back toward Ocean. "I like to drive up the main drag," he explained. "Carmel always reminds me of an elf village in the middle of a forest. I love it."

Kendall responded quickly to his note of pleasure. "Me, too. People are so quick to disparage all this. They don't understand that the townspeople never really meant for it to get so commercial. It just sort of grew, like Topsy. But I doubt if they'll ever give in completely. Still no sidewalks on most of the side streets. No streetlighting to speak of, no proper mail delivery, and there are still lots of artists and writers and craftsmen who make it their home."

"It's still quaint, too," Langston agreed. "The first time I came here, I expected to find neon lights flashing all over the place like you find in most tourist traps. But there was nary a neon. It was positively refreshing after some of the so-called antique villages I've seen."

A companionable silence ensued, and Kendall, after watching for a few moments to see how he handled the car, settled back to enjoy the ride. Like most good drivers, she was a nervous passenger until she had developed faith in another driver's capabilities. But Langston drove with relaxed ease, perfectly at one with his car. They turned up Carpenter Street and headed toward the highway. Once there, he drove fast but without braggadocio. They were on the freeway for only a brief time, however, before he turned off and headed down Munras Avenue through Monterey.

"Where are we going?" she asked.

"The Sardine Factory. I hope you like it."

"I've never eaten there."

"For shame," he scolded lightly, never taking his eyes from the road ahead. "The best restaurant on the Peninsula, and you've never eaten there?"

"I don't know about 'best,'" she contradicted with a smile. "It has a very good reputation, of course, and it's supposed to be the most expensive restaurant in Monterey, but there are more good restaurants in this area than you could count in a month of Sundays."

"Well, I think you'll like it." Fisherman's wharf parking lot sprawled ahead of them with the lights of the Jolly Rogue on the right and the dock lights of the yacht harbor gleaming straight ahead. Langston turned left and drove through the brightly lit tunnel, passing the main wharf with its usual gaily jostling crowd of tourists, and following the shoreline around to Cannery Row. The Sardine Factory was not on the Row itself but a couple of streets up, which made parking easier than it generally was when one went to Neil De Vaughn's, the Outrigger, or one of the other restaurants perched just above the crashing waves.

Langston found a space on the street in front of the Sardine Factory, and they walked up the long ramp to the front door. It looked rather like an old shack from the outside, Kendall thought, and the inside did not impress her very much either. It was clean and neat, of course, with its white-clothed tables and polished paneling. But it was small and seemed crowded. The maître d' appeared as though by magic, however, greeted Langston by name, and quickly showed them to a table at the side of the room. Once they were seated, any sense of being crowded dissipated at once.

"Cocktails, monsieur?"

"Yes," Langston responded promptly. "A gin and tonic for me, and for the lady—"

"The same, please," Kendall said when he paused.

"So you're not a gourmet either," Langston chuckled.

"Not particularly. But what makes you say so?"

"The gin and tonic. Some of my friends go into conniptions when I order one before dinner. They say it ruins the palate, and that one should stick with a light aperitif. In other words, we should be having white wine instead. But I like gin and tonic."

"Me, too." Kendall turned her attention to the menu and was delighted to see that, although abalone was still off, they did serve calamari. Their drinks arrived quickly, and Langston placed their orders, teasing Kendall about hers.

"Squid, for Pete's sake!"

"It's very good. Tastes just like abalone if it's done properly."

"Abalone tastes like abalone. Squid is squid. Didn't they have abalone?"

"Thanks to the otters, the pollution, and the poachers, nobody has abalone these days. It's too expensive even for this place, assuming they could get it at all."

"Shall we try them?"

She stared at him but realized that he was completely in earnest. If she wanted abalone, he would do his best to get it for her. It gave her a rather odd sensation somewhere near the pit of her stomach, but she suppressed it and replied with her customary equanimity, "No, thank you. I like calamari."

"As you wish." He sipped his drink, watching her over the rim of his glass with rather discomfiting directness. "I wonder if you realize how very beautiful you are."

Kendall gave him look for look, for once stifling the ridiculous excitement his words caused without much difficulty. God knew, other men had commented on her beauty, so there was no reason that it should please her overmuch that Langston would do so. Besides, it would never do to let him see that she was vulnerable to his charms. She must handle him as she would handle any other outspoken admirer.

"Of course I do," she replied evenly. "I would have to be blind not to know I'm beautiful. I do what I can to stay that way, too, although there's not much I can do about the nose."

"The nose is perfect," he said, grinning at her again.

"No, it's not, but I suppose you think I'm going to go all fluffy and coquettish just because you flatter me. I won't, you know. I detest flattery." Fearing he might somehow read the contradiction to that statement in her eyes, she reached into her purse, drew out her cigarettes, and tapped one out. Langston picked up a book of matches from the ashtray and lit it for her.

"I didn't know you smoked."

"Do you mind?"

"Not at all. It's not good for your health, of course, but I like my ladies to have a vice or two. Makes them more interesting."

"Mr. Langston," Kendall said, her words dripping sudden frost as her topsy-turvy emotions came to earth with a thud, "I am not one of your ladies. We came here to discuss a business matter. Do you suppose we might get on with it?"

"Later. You might have come because you wanted to talk business, ma'am. I came because I wanted to have dinner with you. And telling you that you are beautiful is not flattery. It is the simple truth."

"To say that my nose is perfect is blatant flattery."

"Touché," he replied, surprising her.

Her own sudden anger had disappeared, and her emotions seemed to have balanced themselves at last. She smiled and began to relax. "Well, at least you don't battle lost causes. I suppose I was rude before. Meg says I usually am when people go on about my looks. I don't mean to be. I just prefer talking about other matters."

"Fair enough. But no business until dessert."

"You're the boss," she replied demurely, then added with a twinkle, "How was the dentist?"

Langston grinned appreciatively. "Guess I asked for that. To tell the truth, he began by terrifying me—blathered something about a possible root canal—but it turned out to be nothing more serious than a cracked filling. Do you want another drink?"

"I don't think so, thank you."

He shook his head at the hovering cocktail waitress, and a moment later, their salads arrived. Langston kept up a patter of small talk, and Kendall began to realize that he knew a great deal about a myriad of subjects. She kept her own end up easily enough, however, and something about his attitude made her feel intelligent to the point of brilliance. It wasn't anything he said particularly; it was just the undivided attention he gave to her every word. Men usually tried to impress her, downplaying her opinions in order to give full play to their own. Jack carried things so far sometimes as to make her feel little more than a fluffy-headed nitwit. But Langston was not only attentive. He listened with respect. And it seemed later as though they had discussed everything under the sun from world politics to the energy crunch to Greenpeace's attempts to save the whale.

The food was excellent. Clearly, the reputation the restaurant had built for itself centered upon its delicious cuisine and outstanding service. But Kendall would not remember the evening for the food alone. The greater part of her energy was focused upon the man sitting opposite her. By the time dessert was offered, she felt completely at ease in his company, and the feeling she had had earlier of having known him all her life was accentuated. He was warm and gentle and full of laughter. He even made her laugh aloud, more than once, and she was not a laughing sort by nature. She had an excellent sense of humor, but she simply wasn't given to loud, sudden bursts of merriment.

"Cheesecake?"

Kendall shook her head. "I'd rather have a grasshopper made with ice cream if they make them here."

He chuckled and glanced inquiringly at their waiter, who

nodded in an almost paternal affirmative. "One crème de menthe milkshake for the lady, and you can bring me some Drambuie spilled gently over a couple of ice cubes." Their drinks came almost immediately, and after a small sip of his, Langston reached into his jacket pocket and withdrew a pipe and tobacco pouch. He proceeded to fill his pipe. "See, I have vices, too."

"Your house didn't smell of pipe smoke."

"It better not, considering the fortune I've spent on dehumidifiers and air purifiers and such like muck. Besides, I usually only indulge myself after dinner or when I'm particularly bored in a meeting."

"You must have all that stuff at your office, too, then. Why aren't there any windows in that place?"

"Security, mostly," he replied.

"So you must produce more than marine supplies," she said slowly. "I wondered, but it didn't seem like a high-security place. Why, I just said I wanted to see you, and the guard at the door let me in without even checking with your office to see if I was expected."

"Seeing me isn't that big a deal," he grinned. "He might have been a tad more inquisitive if you'd asked to see the specs for our latest project or the prototype of a little number one of my plants is about to begin manufacturing for Uncle Sam."

"But how would that one man stop anyone who really wanted to get into the place?"

"It's easier than it looked," he explained. "The whole place is under constant surveillance by closed-circuit television, and the lobby area can be shut off from the rest of the building by the push of a button."

"What if somebody knocks him unconscious before he can push the button?" Kendall wanted to know.

Langston chuckled. "Planning a little raid, are you? It will never work. He doesn't have to push the button. It can be pushed from any number of points, and of course the closed-circuit television is monitored. The monitor can push the button. Simple, see? I've got pretty much the same system at the house," he added.

She had finished her drink and nodded now to the busboy who offered hot coffee. The smell of Langston's pipe smoke drifted to her, reminding her briefly and warmly of long-ago moments spent with her grandfather. She reached for her cigarettes. "If I had something to protect," she said slowly, "I would make it clear to anyone who might want it that it was well protected. I'd have armed guards all over the place."

Langston lit her cigarette. "You'd have made a big hit with my father. When he ran the company, that's the way it was. High fences, lots of uniformed, armed guards, even guard dogs. Alarms, searches, the whole lot. But I'm allergic to overt security measures. They give me the willies. And now that the electronics age is here, it's much easier to be subtle about it."

"But what if somebody pulled the plug on all your gadgetry?"

He shook his head. "The television and the security doors operate on their own power sources. If the lights go out, the doors close automatically and the television switches to infrared coverage. We had an electrical storm a month or so ago, and the lights went out. We couldn't do a thing until the backup generator came on because there's no way to open the doors until the master computer says everything is clear. And," he added with a smile, "we have just come to the end of what I can tell you. The rest is classified."

"How classified do you get out there, for heaven's sake?"

"Most of our stuff is just labeled Secret, but we do have some top-secret projects, and one or two that go beyond that."

"Beyond top secret! I thought that was the pinnacle—or is there really an 'eyes-only' category like in the James Bond books."

Langston chuckled again. "There is, indeed, oh doubting one. There is also a vast forest of classifications in between.

I've got guys working for me who've got security clearances that are themselves classified. Nutty, isn't it?"

"But then, you must have a pretty high clearance yourself," Kendall said. "Can you tell me what it is?"

"I could, but it wouldn't mean much without an explanation, and I couldn't give the explanation without teetering on forbidden territory. Since you've brought it up, however, there is something you probably should know." She looked curious, and Langston's color rose self-consciously. "Nothing will happen, of course, but if by some stroke of ill luck we should ever have an accident and you come out of it better than I do, the first thing you must do is get in touch with Sylvia or Jerry. I'll give you private numbers for both of them. If you can't call one of them yourself, get the cops to do it."

"But what could Sylvia do that I can't?"

"She would contact the security people at Fort Ord. She knows who to call and precisely what to tell them. There's this stupid rule that I can't be given anesthetic without someone there to make sure I don't spill any beans. Had my wisdom teeth pulled, and because of the way I respond to dentists, they had to put me clear under. It was downright embarrassing at the time, believe me. But that's enough about me. Speaking of Sylvia, I guess now's as good a time as any to talk business."

So Kendall explained the problem at last. Langston listened attentively, asking a question or two, and then declared flatly, "You don't think you can get along with Sylvia."

Kendall favored him with a direct look, irritated because he seemed to be placing the blame for the problem at her door. "I can get along with her if necessary, but I cannot let her do the job you hired me to do. If you want her to select the colors for your house, say so, and I'll bow out. If not, then you'll have to explain matters to her. You wouldn't put her in charge of a government project and expect your engineers to submit to her design decisions; you shouldn't give her any

more scope in a project like this one. Not when you've paid
out good money to experts to see the job done properly."

"Do you want me to send her to Timbuktu?"

She looked amused. "I hardly think that will be necessary.
We do need someone we can contact when you are unavail-
able. There will be a number of things that will need your
approval before we go ahead with them. But it should be
your approval, not hers. I doubt if she was planning to hover
over us at the Sandcastle, but she does need to understand
how the color business works so she won't try to influence
you to choose her colors instead of your own."

"Okay. I'll speak to her. Are you ready to leave?"

She nodded, feeling almost deflated by the ease with which
she had won her point. But she cheered up again when he
steered her past the car and down the hill toward Cannery
Row.

"The night's still young enough. How about a stroll to work
off some of that dinner?"

They walked past the noisy Warehouse and down to the
Cannery, where some of the shops were still open and doing
good business. But the air was chilly, and it was not long
before it became obvious that unless they went inside somewhere, it would soon be uncomfortably so. Langston nodded
across the street toward the Outrigger. They've got a pretty
quiet bar. How about another drink before we go?" She
agreed to it, and in a matter of moments they were sitting
companionably across from one another again. Conversation
drifted from subject to subject as it had done before, and
Kendall soon found herself telling him about her family.

"My father was the stiffly upright, civilized sort," she told
him. "He always wanted things just so, and blew his stack if
they didn't suit him. My brother George is just like him.
Mother was a hypochondriac until Daddy died. Then suddenly all her aches and pains disappeared, and now she trav-
els all over the world and thoroughly enjoys being the merry
widow."

"Just the one brother?"

"Yes, thank heavens. Two or more like George, and I'd have been a basket case before my teens."

"I've got two brothers and three sisters," Langston said with a grin. "My family is the loud, demonstrative sort, with everybody mixing in everybody else's business. We're scattered all over the world now, but we still keep in touch and give each other advice, solicited or not."

"Meg's family's like that, too," Kendall said, returning his smile. "They are lots of fun, but I must confess that I prefer the occasional odd moment of peace and quiet."

"Don't try to make me believe you're the hermit type," he chuckled. But the warm look in his eyes made it clear that he wasn't laughing at her. Kendall had the distinct feeling that he was truly interested. He wanted to know what made her tick. If she were to tell him that she *was* a hermit, he would want to know the hows and whys of it. He would really want to understand.

She smiled. "Not a hermit, perhaps, although there are times when my friends might disagree. Sometimes I just need space and time to myself. Days of it. I take long walks on the beach, or I curl up in front of the fire with a good long book and don't answer my phone. Now it's a fairly easy thing to accomplish, but when I was a kid, it was more difficult. Then I used to sleep. For days at a time. After finals at school I'd come home and go to bed. My mother would bring food at mealtimes and I'd wake up enough to eat some, but mostly I just slept. It was my way of escaping from the world for a time."

"But you'd miss whole chunks of life that way!" he protested.

"Don't you ever need to be alone?"

"Of course I do. Everyone does. But I couldn't bear days of it. I'd go berserk. When I need to revitalize myself, I exercise or I change my routine, but I like to have people around to talk to, to exchange ideas with."

He continued to probe into her thoughts and feelings, comparing them with his own philosophy of life until they had finished their second round of drinks. After that, they wandered back up the hill to his car. But conversation between them continued to flow easily all the way back to Carmel. For once, Kendall felt as though she was making a friend without passing through that initial period of wary distrust. Something deep within her seemed to reach out to him as though to a kindred spirit. It was a warm and cozy feeling. She directed Langston to her house and explained how she had come to live there. Parking on the beachside of the road, he opened her door, and helped her out, glancing across the street at the little carport dug into the hill.

"This is where Carmel could use some modern streetlighting. Where's your front door, for Pete's sake?"

"Through the gate. It's a side door, actually."

"Through the gate!" Disapproval rang in his voice. "I don't suppose you've got so much as a lock on that gate or a dog to watch the place either."

"No." She grinned at his tone. "How could I keep a dog? Meg and I often go away for a weekend or longer on buying trips for clients. Who would feed it?"

"I don't know, but this is ridiculous," he said sternly as he pushed open the squeaking gate. It was pitch black in the walkway. "Do you come home to this often?" he asked with an ominous note in his voice.

"I left the outside light on when I left," she said calmly. "It must have burned out. I'll admit it used to give me the creeps when I first moved here, but nothing awful's ever happened, and I'm quite comfortable with it now."

"Have you got some oil and a fresh light bulb?" he asked bluntly.

Kendall was fumbling in her purse for her keys. "Yes, of course."

"Fine. I'll change it for you and fix that gate. Give me those things before you drop them. You should carry a flashlight in that bag. For that matter, why the devil didn't you leave a light or two on inside when you left?"

"There's still an energy crunch, remember?"

"Humph." Taking the keys from her, he unlocked the door, and she reached for the light switch. The warm glow lit the living room.

"The light bulbs and oil are in the kitchen," she said.

"This is very nice. Your handiwork?"

"Yes. Make yourself at home." He seemed willing to take her at her word, and Kendall hurried into the kitchen to get one of the yellow bug-repellent light bulbs she used in the outside fixtures and a tin of three-in-one oil. He smiled down at her when she handed them to him, then turned back toward the door.

He oiled the gate first, then without so much as standing on his tiptoes, he reached up and unscrewed first the nubbled-glass fixture, which she took away to wash, and then the bulb itself. When Kendall brought him the clean fixture, he replaced it just as easily. If she had done it herself, she realized, she would have had to drag out the stepladder, and the little step up to the door made setting that up a precarious venture, to say the least. It was with deep sincerity that she thanked him for attending to the matter.

"I had a wonderful evening, Steve," she said then. "Thank you very much."

"Not throwing me out already, are you," he teased, moving to take her in his arms. His touch seemed to flash electrically through her, and she trembled slightly as she looked up into his eyes to see what she might read there. But his eyelids drooped, shadowing their expression, and he lowered his head, his lips pressing first gently, then more demandingly, against hers. It was as though she had been dropped into a warm but violent whirlpool. There was a sensation as though she were falling and couldn't stop herself. Then it seemed as though she had come home to something warm and wonderful. One moment her heart seemed perfectly still; the next, it was pounding like a stormy sea against a rugged coast. She began to respond to his kiss. It seemed perfectly natural to feel his hands caressing her, gently moving over the soft cashmere of her dress as he embraced her. Then she realized that one hand had reached the zipper at the back of her neck, and she felt a soft tug.

CHAPTER 5

"No, Steve." Kendall was breathless. And he must not have heard her, because his hand did not even hesitate. The zipper began to give. She stiffened and tried to pull away, managing to keep her voice cool in spite of everything. "I said no, Steve, and I meant it. I think you'd better go now. It's getting late, and we both have to work tomorrow."

"But I want to take you to bed."

Kendall felt as though her heart had stopped. "What did you say?"

"You heard me," he murmured gruffly, pulling her closer. She stared up at him, her feelings a mixture of shock, bewildered disillusionment, resentment, and indignation, as well as a passionate longing deeper and more stirring than anything she had ever felt for any other man. Such was her stupor that she made no effort to elude him as his lips claimed hers again. And then, her eyes seemed to close of their own volition, and it was back into the whirlpool, her body responding to his touch in spite of herself, as desire reached a fever pitch. One of his hands gently caressed her breast, and she strained against him, her lips softening, then parting as his kisses became more demanding.

His hand left her breast and she felt the telltale, gentle tug at her zipper again. Part of her wanted to let him go ahead, but her better self said the time had come to call a halt before things got completely out of hand. Nonetheless, it would be difficult. She felt as though her own will had simply melted away, leaving her a near-willing victim to his every ploy. Fighting the sense of overwhelming languor, she opened her eyes to encounter that devilish twinkle glinting above her. At that moment, however, Langston's grasp on her zipper became firmer, more confident. It was enough. She brought both hands up to push hard against his chest, and surprised, he relaxed his grip.

"I'm sorry, Steve." It was barely a whisper. She took a deep breath to steady her agitated nerves and looked at him more directly. "I had a good time tonight, but I hardly know you, and I'm not going to bed with you."

"Oh, come on, Kendall," he said irritably. "I hate games. You're a grown woman, not a child, and I know you like me well enough."

"I might be an adult," she returned coolly, "but not a consenting one, my friend. I will not go to bed with you. This might come as a shock, but I have certain principles, and liking you is not sufficient reason to break one of the strongest of them."

He looked down at her, his hands still on her shoulders. "Are you trying to tell me that someone who looks like you do is still . . . well, you know . . . still . . . damn it, girl, you're putting me on, and I won't have it! You're just trying that old chestnut of playing hard to get. But I'm not the fellow to fall for it. I expect a square deal."

"You also seem to *expect* lovemaking, Mr. Langston," Kendall retorted sarcastically, well and truly angry now. "Do all your *ladies* put out for you? Is it the payment you demand for such favors as taking them to dinner or changing their light bulbs? Because if it is, you picked the wrong pigeon this time. You can believe what you like about my reasons, but I can't think of a single thing I've said or done tonight that should lead you to believe I'd go to bed with you. Nothing beyond your own incredible ego could make you think I'd just hop under the covers at the mere lifting of your eyebrow. I told you before that this evening was strictly business. That's how it was, and that's how it stays. Good night, sir!"

She stepped away from him and moved to open the door, then shot him a look of icy challenge. Frowning angrily, Langston opened his mouth as if to bellow, but encountering the glacial look in those gray green eyes, he hesitated. Then, without a word, he snapped his mouth shut and moved past her and out the door. A brief moment later, she heard the gate slam. Then there was silence until it was broken by the roar of the Datsun's engine and a slight—very slight—squeal of tires as he drove away.

Kendall shut the door with exaggerated gentleness, locked it, and let out a long sigh. But it was not relief that she felt; it was much more a sense of depression. Men were so dreadfully predictable. Even a man like Langston. How could she have thought for a moment that he would prove to be any different from the rest of them? And she! To think she had very nearly lost her temper with him! As though she had never been propositioned before. Usually, she managed to laugh such things off, to keep similar situations on an even keel. When she had played nearly the same scene on one of their first dates with Jack—and numerous others before him —she had kept things amusing, lighthearted; and, although she had had to be particularly firm in some cases, she had always managed to part on friendly terms with the gentlemen in question. But it was more than that. Never before had she doubted the validity of her principles.

The thought struck without warning. She moved away from the door, down the hall to her bedroom, turning the traitorous notion over and over in her mind. She had thought she knew herself inside out and had decided long since that she must know a man well and care for him deeply before she would agree to share a physical experience with him. There had to be something special, a serious commitment, a possibility at least that the relationship might lead to marriage. Surely, there had not been time enough to discover whether that commitment would form a part of her relationship with Stephen Langston. But now, suddenly, she felt as though her own body threatened to betray her. For it had not been Langston's declaration that had infuriated her, she realized bitterly. It had been, instead, her own immediate and overwhelming desire to let him have his way. It had been, in fact, almost as if she had wanted him to overrule her, to make her respond in spite of herself. But surely she would have hated him if he had forced her to comply willingly to his desires. And how could such a thing be, anyway? It was a contradiction in terms. How could willingness possibly be forced. It was absurd, that's what it was.

She switched on her radio, hoping to turn her thoughts in a new direction. It was tuned, as usual, to a mood-music station and something that sounded like Mantovani drifted into the bedroom. Humming softly, she slipped out of the cashmere dress and into a soft blue velvet robe. But in spite of the radio, her thoughts kept turning back to Langston. What *would* have happened if he had said nothing, if he had simply held her and kissed her and gently caressed her until her passions had rendered her incapable of rational thought? Would she have given in? Would her faithless body have been the willing accomplice to his purpose? And why did she so badly want to know the answers to those questions? Was it because she hoped she would have been strong enough to stick to her principles? Or was it because she hoped she would not?

"Stop it, Kendall!" she said aloud. "What you need, my girl, is a good shaking. And a cup of hot chocolate." She hung up her dress and moved purposefully toward the kitchen. She had been acting like a moonstruck adolescent, and it was time to grow up again. Firmly keeping her mind on her work, she put the bright red kettle on the burner and reached into one cupboard for the cocoa, into another for a mug. Then, needing something to occupy her hands until the water boiled, she got out her big sponge and the cleanser, cleared the counters, and began to scrub. They didn't really need it, but dust and grease did tend to accumulate in corners, and every little bit of attention helped. She timed it well and was just putting the little spice basket back in place when the whistle began its first, tentative screech. Quickly, she turned off the gas and made her cocoa, adding two tablespoons of peppermint schnapps to the finished product.

Then she decided to enjoy her drink with a final cigarette before she washed her face and went to bed.

The brisk exercise had helped. Her mind felt perfectly clear again when she sat down at the kitchen table and lit her cigarette. Now perhaps she would be able to think objectively. Langston's charms had obviously had a devastating effect upon her, but surely she would have been able to handle him no matter how he had approached her. Without a doubt, she had lost her equanimity only because of the shockingly direct manner he had used. It had been typical of him, of course. He thought he had only to make his wishes known to see them gratified. That he was used to having his own way was blindingly obvious. His very confidence seemed to sweep all obstacles aside, and it was probably the cause of her own self-doubts. But, whatever the reason, she had herself under control now. She had shown him where she stood, so now they ought to be able to get on with the job at hand without any personal distractions. Admittedly, the idea was a bit depressing, but she could deal with that, too.

The phone rang, startling her out of her reverie. There was an extension on the wall near the table, so she reached out and lifted the receiver, half expecting to hear heavy breathing on the other end. It was nearly midnight.

"So, you're home at last." The familiar voice sounded a bit on the sulky side, she thought.

"Hello, Jack. Checking up on me?" Her tone was cool.

"Just wanted to be sure you got home safely," he replied. "How was your evening? Or am I premature?"

Stifling the resentment that rose automatically in response to the last question, Kendall forced herself to speak calmly. "The evening was pleasant enough," she said. "At least we got that little problem I mentioned earlier worked out."

"That's good. Tell me about it."

"Some other time, Jack, if you don't mind. I've got a busy schedule tomorrow, and it's almost midnight. I was just getting ready to go to bed."

"Alone, I trust." She didn't answer, and after a brief, chilly silence, he sighed. "All right, I shouldn't have said that. It was uncalled for. Forgive me?"

"Call me tomorrow," she said evenly. "I really need to get some sleep."

He was clearly reluctant to hang up, and Kendall knew that he wanted some sort of reassurance from her, but she felt unable to cope with him at the moment. He protested briefly, but when he realized that he was only annoying her, he said good night. She replaced the receiver, glaring at it.

"Men!"

She rinsed out her mug and the ashtray, switched out the lights in the kitchen and living room, washed her face, and went to bed. It seemed as if she had barely fallen asleep before the phone rang again. But while she struggled blearily to rub sleep away, she caught a glimpse of the glowing hands on the little clock near the phone. It was four o'clock in the morning! The birdlike little bell chirruped again. Slowly, she reached to answer it. Who in the world could be calling at such an hour? Emergency? The heavy breather she had expected earlier? Her mother in Europe, forgetting the time difference? The last possibility was a comforting one, and her hand gripped the receiver more firmly.

"Hello." Her voice slurred, and she straightened a little in bed, trying to wake herself up.

"Hi, Kendall. It's Steve."

He sounded totally awake and alert, and she found the sound of his deep voice even more unsettling than usual. She glanced at the clock again. "Do you know what time it is?"

There was a pause. "It's a little after four. Why?"

"Where are you?" Now, there's a bright question, she informed herself. Where would he be at four in the morning, except home in bed like any other civilized person?

"At the office. I had some things to do."

"At 4:00 A.M.!"

"It's a great time. Very few interruptions. I get twice as much accomplished as I do in the daytime."

"When do you sleep?"

"Don't need much. More than Henry Kissinger, though," he admitted, and she thought she could detect a tinge of regret in his tone at the idea that he wasn't quite the human dynamo the erstwhile secretary of state had reputedly been. "I hear he only sleeps about two hours a night. I need at least twice that. But I didn't call to chat about my habits."

"Didn't you?" She had herself under control again, and her tone was slightly amused.

"No. I called to apologize. I was way out of line tonight, and you were perfectly right to give me my walking papers. Guess I should think myself lucky that you only ordered me out of the house and didn't knock me from here to next Christmas instead."

"I don't hit people," Kendall said, repressing a chuckle at the brief, absurd mental image of herself launching someone his size into orbit. Despite her efforts, a small gurgle escaped her lips, and Langston heard it. He heaved a deep sigh of relief.

"You're not still mad at me." It was a statement, not a question.

"No." She wasn't, nor was she angry at his choosing such an odd hour for his apology, although he seemed totally oblivious to the possibility that she might have found being wakened at four in the morning slightly irritating.

"Good. I've got piles of work and innumerable appointments lined up for the rest of the week, but if I declare a holiday Saturday, will you drive down to Big Sur with me?"

"Why Big Sur?" she asked, trying to ignore the sudden, ridiculous pounding of her heart.

"Because I like the drive," he said with a laugh. "I thought about telling you that I had business down there, or that I wanted to discuss some small matter about the house, but I was afraid I'd blow it later by forgetting all about whatever it was I had told you. Then I'd just be in trouble again. So it seemed the best thing would be to tell the truth, that I want to drive down there with you. What about it?"

Tell him no dice! said her better self sharply.

"I'd be delighted, Steve," said Kendall. "What time?"

"I'll let you know," he replied. "A lot will depend upon whether I can swing it for the whole day or not. This is a pretty busy place these days."

"That will be fine," she said.

"Good. There's just one other thing, and then I've got to get back to work." He hesitated, and Kendall found herself suppressing an urge to apologize for keeping him. "I hope you won't go all icy on me again, but I'm going to send a couple of guys out tomorrow to install a photoelectric cell to control your outside lights."

"A what!"

"A photoelectric cell. That's a device that—"

"I know what it is," she interrupted. "But why on earth—"

"Because it's not safe for you to come home to a dark house, that's why. Not *that* dark house, at any rate. Not with that pitch-black walkway. The way that guest house blocks even moonlight from the rear, anyone could be hiding in there, and unless the moon was directly overhead, you'd have no way of knowing till he had you. And nobody would be the wiser. A prowler could do whatever he liked completely unseen from the street. You should have a lock on that gate, too, but at least with a photoelectric cell, when the sun goes down, the lights will come on. Don't argue with me, Kendall," he added on a note of sternness. "Not where your safety is at stake."

"I won't," she said. "It's a terrific idea. I'll admit I forget to leave the light on as often as not when I go out before it gets dark, and I can never bring myself to leave it on all day even when I know I'll get home after dark. This way, I can save the energy, and there will always be a light on when I come home. But I don't see why you should send your men. I'm perfectly capable of attending to the matter myself."

"It's already been taken care of," he declared flatly, "and it's not that I don't trust you to do it, so don't climb back onto that high horse of yours. I just want to be sure it's done right away, and no matter what sort of connections you have, you'd very likely have to wait a day or two at the very least before anyone could get around to it."

It was true. She'd be lucky not to have to wait a week or more. "Okay, but I insist upon paying for it. I can't let you foot the bill. It just wouldn't be right."

"More principles, Kendall?" But now he sounded amused.

"If you want to put it that way."

"Fair enough. I'll let you know what it costs. Now I really do have to get back to work. I'll call again later in the week. Good night."

"Good night, Steve." She replaced the receiver and lay back against her pillows with a tiny smile tugging at her lips and a mellow glow spreading through her body. It was a rather odd sensation to know that someone else was looking out for her welfare. She was accustomed to taking care of herself, and nearly everyone she knew had been well trained to leave her to it. But there was something very pleasant about the way Langston had taken the matter of her safety upon his own shoulders. Perhaps she could even grow accustomed to letting someone else take care of her. The thought lingered, warming her from her toes all the way up, and as she drifted back to sleep, she wondered how it was that she could have been so furious with him earlier when a simple phone call in the middle of the night could make her feel so good.

His men arrived before she left for the studio the next morning. There were two of them, one burly and bearded and the other small and wiry, but both exuded a confident air of competence. They presented identification cards, and the larger man gave her a note from Langston as well, confirming that they were the men he had told her to expect.

"He certainly didn't leave anything to chance, did he?" Kendall commented dryly after reading the note.

"No, ma'am," replied the bearded man. "Mr. Langston never does. Is there already a light out back?"

"Out back?"

"Yes, ma'am. Mr. Langston wants a cell installed there, too. It will be easier if there's already a fixture back there."

"Well, there is, but it really lights only the pathway to the guest house." She regarded the men searchingly. "I'm beginning to get the feeling that Mr. Langston intends to see this place lit up like a used-car lot. It's only fair to warn you that I would have the strongest objections to such a plan. What exactly are your orders?"

The smaller man cleared his throat suddenly and looked away, but the man who had been doing all the talking chuckled openly. "Seems you know the boss pretty well, Miss Blake. But I think he realized you'd feel that way. He told us to light this walkway and the carport bright enough so's he could read the fine print on a government contract at midnight, but to stick to proper garden lighting in the back."

"And what exactly does Mr. Langston mean by 'proper garden lighting,' Mr. Donnelly?" Kendall asked suspiciously, remembering his name from the identification card.

He grinned. "Depends on what we find back there. How 'bout a tour?"

They followed the walkway around to the little, ivy-walled back garden. It was filled with shrubs of all sorts, and somewhere nearby a flicker was beating a staccato tattoo while he searched out his breakfast. The little guest cottage, straight back from the walkway and some twenty feet from the kitchen door, looked like something out of *Hansel and Gretel*, backed as it was by tall Monterey pines and nearly hidden from sight by the thick shrubbery. Donnelly shook his head.

"Beautiful little place, Miss Blake, but a haven for a prowler. We'll string some back-lighting through that shrubbery. It'll look real nice when it's lit up, and it oughta make anyone think twice before creeping around in there. The light on the path looks okay, but I think we'd best put another one over your patio."

"But that would shine right into my bedroom at night!" Kendall protested.

"Thicker drapes, maybe?" he suggested. She glared at him. "Okay, then we'll angle it so it only lights the patio. But you really do need another one back here, Miss Blake."

"Very well. I suppose it's useless to argue with you. What else did he order?"

"Well, I brought a couple of timers for the living-room lights. They're the variable type, so the lights won't go on at exactly the same time every day, but you won't ever have to walk into a dark house."

"What else?" she asked grimly, beginning to get Langston's measure, and not at all sure she liked it.

"That's all . . . except for the locks."

"Good grief! What locks?"

"Deadbolts for the front and kitchen doors and orders to check all the windows to see what's needed and provide it. Uh, he also wants a deadbolt put on that gate up front."

"I see. When will the full alarm system be installed?"

Donnelly laughed out loud at her sarcastic tone, and even the smaller man allowed himself a hearty chuckle. "Don't think it didn't occur to him, Miss Blake. But he said you'd throw a fit."

"He was right. I'm tempted to throw one anyway," she informed him. He shot a speaking glance at his companion, then looked back at her. "Oh, don't worry, Mr. Donnelly. You won't be the target. I realize you've got to follow orders, and I realize, too, that if I send you away, you'll have to listen to him read you the riot act. But I shall certainly have a thing or two to say to Mr. Langston about this high-handedness of his. Believe me."

"I don't doubt it," Donnelly replied, smiling again. "Thanks for your consideration, Miss Blake. Don't mind telling you I was beginning to think we'd be tossed out on our ears, and I wasn't looking forward to reporting to Mr. Langston if that happened."

Kendall relaxed, returning his smile with a small one of her own. "I've got to go to work," she said. "Can I put a pot of coffee on for you before I go?"

"That would be real nice, Miss Blake. We ought to have a key, too, if you've got an extra one. We'll drop it by your studio along with the new ones when we're done here."

With a sigh of exasperated resignation, Kendall detached her house key from her key ring and handed it to him. It never occurred to her that she might not be able to trust these two men in her house. Langston would not have sent anyone who wasn't completely reliable. She started the coffee, grabbed her coat and purse, and set out for Meg's cottage, some three blocks up the hill. Really, she thought, as she stepped briskly into the crisp, sunlit morning, talk about giving a man an inch! And Langston seemed to know just how many steps of his mile he could take before she would balk. If he had mentioned all his plans on the phone, she would have told him to go fly a large kite. But he had told her just enough to insure her cooperation. He had probably known, too, that she would hesitate to subject his workmen to a display of his temper if she could avoid it. And perhaps he'd thought that if he could get the workmen in the front door, she would say no more about it. Well, he was wrong about that!

Meg greeted her cheerfully upon her arrival, demanding to know how her evening had gone. Kendall looked at her blankly. The evening itself seemed somehow long past. But she gathered her wits quickly enough.

"I think he will speak to Miss Hutton," she said. "He seemed to understand the problem once it was fully explained. We'll still have to work with her, of course, but she won't have the power to make the final decisions."

"Well, I can handle Miss Hutton," Meg declared confidently. "But what was it like? Where did you go?"

Kendall told her, keeping her tone strictly matter-of-fact and sticking to the plain details of their evening. But when she mentioned that he had disapproved of her unlocked gate and unlit walkway, her tone sharpened, and Meg looked at her more carefully. Kendall noticed the look and forced her voice to behave itself, but she glossed over the rest, merely saying that Langston had departed soon after taking her home. "Then Jack called," she added with a tiny smile.

But Meg was not so easily distracted from the scent. "You're leaving something out," she accused as they headed for the Camaro. "I know you, Kendall Blake, and there's something you don't want to tell me. Surely, you weren't idiotic enough to get into an argument with Steve over that stupid gate! I've told you a hundred times how dangerous that entry is. And if you left the light off again, no wonder he didn't like it!"

Kendall turned the key in the ignition, and the engine started with its usual throbbing purr. She turned to look fondly at Meg, her eyes gleaming with amusement. "It isn't so much that he didn't like it as what he decided to do about it," she said, making a U-turn to head toward the studio. On the way, she explained about the workmen, knowing full well that Meg would not share her indignation in the matter. Meg didn't.

"How utterly magnificent!" she declared, laughing. "How absolutely, incredibly magnificent!"

"How incredibly high-handed!" Kendall retorted. "The man has no sense of what is suitable. He's got no right to interfere like this. I can take perfectly good care of myself, and I don't need him making decisions about how I should live!"

"Well, at least he puts his money where his mouth is," Meg pointed out practically. "This sounds like it's going to cost him a small fortune."

Kendall went perfectly still, her face draining of all expression. They had pulled up in front of the studio, and she switched off the engine, then turned to look at Meg. "I told him I'd pay for it. In fact, I insisted upon it."

Meg's eyes widened. "You're kidding! How did you manage to do that if you didn't even know what he had planned?"

Kendall waited until they were inside the studio before she explained. But when she had finished, Meg smiled at her. "Goose," she said affectionately, "I doubt if he means to charge you for anything other than the photoelectric cells. At least, that's what it sounds like to me. He may add the time it takes those guys to hook them up, but I bet that's all. Sounds like the canny sort, your Mr. Langston does."

"He's not *my* Mr. Langston!" Kendall flashed. "Oh, hang the man! You're probably right, but I can't let him get away with it. I'm going to call and give him a piece of my mind right now." Meg only smiled as she disappeared tactfully into the workroom, but Kendall ignored her and went to place the call while her temper was still hot. Her fingers practically snapping, she punched out the number for Langston Industries.

"Good morning. Langston Industries," said a brightly cheerful voice.

"Mr. Langston, please," Kendall said crisply.

"One moment. I'll connect you with his office."

"Mr. Langston's office. May I help you?" It was Sandra Welch.

"Mr. Langston, please," Kendall repeated.

"Who's calling, please?"

"Kendall Blake."

"Oh, I'm terribly sorry, Miss Blake, but Mr. Langston is in a very important conference right now. Shall I take a message?"

Feeling slightly deflated, Kendall left her number and rang off. Meg came in from the workroom. "What did he say?"

"He's in conference," Kendall replied with a touch of sarcasm.

"Can't say that I blame him," Meg chuckled. "Safest place for him to be at the moment. Not that he seems to be the least bit cowardly, mind you. Just sensible."

Kendall shot her a speaking look but did not attempt to pursue the matter, and after Meg had checked through her gear to make sure she would have everything she would need, they left for the Sandcastle.

"I was going to check his wardrobe today," Kendall said in the car, "but the way I feel right now, I'm likely to throw out everything but his hair shirts. And don't say he won't have any, because then I'd feel obligated to order some!"

Meg grinned at her. "If you're really that unsettled, we can just do a basic color scheme today, and you can help me with the floor plans and furniture inventory."

They discovered upon their arrival that Miss Hutton had left word that she would telephone later to see if anything was needed; evidently, she had no intention of visiting the house that day. Kendall was relieved. She had not looked forward to the first confrontation with Sylvia Hutton after Langston had spoken to her.

They went quickly to work. Meg seemed to grow more and more excited with each room they visited. "This house is wonderful!" she exclaimed. "It will be perfect for the colors we want to use. How could that woman even have considered firing it up with oranges and golds?" The only room she seemed unsure of was the study. She looked inquiringly at Kendall after her first glimpse of it. "Are you sure he wants us to muck about with this?"

"Miss Hutton said the whole house," Kendall pointed out. "And he certainly didn't say anything to the contrary."

Meg waved a hand at the littered desk. "Well, he's going to have to sort that lot out, because it sure doesn't look as though he allows the maids to clean in here. The carpet has been vacuumed, of course, but everything else looks as though someone flicks a feather duster over it once a year whether it needs it or not."

Kendall chuckled, but she had to admit that Meg was right. The study did have a private feeling about it. It was also a man's room, warm and cozy, and she thought personally that there would be little they could do to improve upon it. Of course, it could stand a little polish, perhaps a new carpet, new drapes, some paint. "We'll ask Miss Hutton what to do about it. That's exactly the sort of thing she should handle for us. Shall we start with the living room?"

They spent the next hour or so moving methodically from room to room. Meg sketched while Kendall drew up a furniture inventory, and while they worked, they exchanged thoughts about possible color schemes. Meg had decided when she first entered the huge, airy living room that it should be decorated in colors from mother-of-pearl.

"He'll like that," Kendall said. "And I think it's a wonderful idea. We'll have to go lightly with the pink tints though, or he'll have a stroke."

"Don't worry. I already thought of that. We'll stick to silver and ice blue for the main effect, with a touch of sea green just to draw the forest a little closer. Then, we can use a painting or two, maybe a sunset with pink tones, and conch shells or something like that for accessories. That will pick up our pink without sending Steve 'round the bend."

"Sounds good," Kendall applauded, adding that they could carry into an emerald green or royal blue in some of the accessories, wherever a splash of color might perk up a corner. Giving her an odd look, Meg pointed out that those were winter shades rather than summer; but, other than that, she neither agreed nor disagreed with the suggestion, and the subject was dropped.

Kendall soon grew tired of listing furniture, so when one of the maids offered to help, she accepted gratefully. "I'm going upstairs, Meg," she said.

"Fine. I'll be ready to stop for lunch in about half an hour. Shall we invite ourselves to Hilda's? She'd be delighted."

"Sure," Kendall agreed. "I'll call now and warn her that we're coming."

"Good idea." Meg went back to her drawing, and Kendall wandered up to the master bedroom, sure that she would find a phone there. It was on the table by the bed. She dialed and a moment later was informing Hilda Quick of the good fortune in store for her. Hilda was as approving as Meg had said she would be. Kendall hung up and stared at the phone for a moment before she picked it up again.

Feeling like an idiot, she called Langston Industries again, only to be told that Mr. Langston had stepped out momentarily but had been given her earlier message. Kendall replied that she was no longer at her studio but at the Sand-castle, that she would be in and out all afternoon, and that perhaps it would be better if Mr. Langston were to call her after five. Sandra Welch agreed cheerfully to pass the message along, and Kendall hung up, feeling as though she had handled a potentially sticky call rather well.

She was certain now that he was avoiding her. It had been entirely possible earlier that he had indeed been in a conference, but he was out of it now, and he had not called. She knew perfectly well that if he had called the office only to be told that she was out, he would have called the Sandcastle next even if Sally had neglected to tell him where she was. He was no doubt giving her a chance to cool off before he spoke with her. Well, live and learn, my friend, she thought to herself. She would not cool off; she would smolder. She would make a point of it.

CHAPTER 6

The next two days passed quickly with both young women finding themselves as busy as they could wish to be. Langston didn't return Kendall's call, but she refused to phone him again. She would just wait. By the same token, although Jack did call, twice, she made excuses not to meet him, knowing he would just create a scene over her dinner date with Langston. He would find out about Saturday soon enough. Let him blow off steam about everything at once, she decided.

Friday morning, she finished her inventory of Langston's wardrobe and made a list of the things he would need to fill it out. Sylvia Hutton entered the room just as she was adding the final items. It was the first time Kendall had seen her since their initial confrontation. Sylvia was cool but very polite. She took the list when Kendall handed it to her.

"This looks all right," she said evenly, after scanning it briefly. "I'll check with Steve and see if he will approve it, but I see no reason why he wouldn't. By the way, Miss Potter mentioned that the painters are ready to begin the study."

Kendall nodded, rather startled by the sudden change of subject. "I think, actually, that Meg intends to begin there simply because she doesn't mean to change much. The colors will remain the same as they are now, although she will order a new carpet, new drapes, and perhaps some new upholstery. I didn't realize that she meant to begin painting so soon, however."

"Well, she said something about the painting contractor having a team idle as of Monday. The study will have to be tidied up; however, I certainly don't have the time to do it, and I know Steve won't get around to it. He won't let the maids touch anything in there either, as you've probably deduced for yourself. But I'm sure, if you're careful not to lose anything, he won't object if you do it for him, Miss Blake. If you wouldn't mind, of course."

She lifted an inquiring eyebrow, and Kendall wondered briefly if Sylvia had any idea how much work she already had to do. But the study did have to be tidied up before the painters came, or they would make a real mess of things, and she really didn't mind. She remembered that there were quite a lot of papers on the desk, but she could stack them in a box until Langston could go through and sort them himself. It wouldn't take long at all, and she wondered briefly why Sylvia didn't do it herself. Then it occurred to her that the ambitious Miss Hutton was probably taking this small opportunity to assert herself as "project commander." Deciding that it could do no harm to humor the woman, Kendall agreed to attend to the matter before she left for the day.

There was much to be accomplished before she could deal with the study, however, so it was late in the afternoon before she began. The bookshelves needed to be cleared, and the whole place needed a thorough dusting, so she called Nelly, the younger of the two maids, to help her, setting the girl to work on the bookshelves, while she herself straightened out all the papers on the desk and a nearby side table. Nelly managed to find some boxes, and Kendall simply stacked everything neatly without trying to categorize anything. Her mind was not strictly upon her work, however. She still longed for an opportunity to tell Langston exactly what she thought of his behavior, for although she had to admit that it was nice to go home to a well-lighted house, the gate had proved to be another matter entirely.

She had not really considered the matter when Donnelly and his sidekick had left her house key and two duplicates at the office with Sally Hunt. But she discovered when she got home that, not only would she have to let herself *in* at the gate with the key, but out as well. The solid wood front door had an inside bolt that she could turn, but both the kitchen door—which had windowpanes in the upper half—and the gate had been fitted with locks that had to be opened with a key from either side. The men had obligingly rekeyed the old locks, so that at least one key fit everything, but it was still a pain in the neck, and she could hardly wait to tell Langston what she thought of it all.

Once she had cleared the desk, she decided to give Nelly a hand, and thus it was that she was standing on a stepladder, her arms loaded with books, when the study door opened suddenly. She turned, startled, to see Langston himself standing upon the threshold, a heavy frown gathering on his face.

"What the devil!" he exclaimed. Nelly looked alarmed, but Kendall met his eyes calmly, despite the fact that his expression sent a cold shiver racing down her spine and made her feel a trifle weak at the knees.

"Did you want anything in particular, Mr. Langston?" she asked, forcing herself to speak in an even tone.

He shot her a speaking look, but his first words were directed to the silent, wide-eyed maid. "You may go, Nelly." She slipped past him with a look of such relief that Kendall nearly smiled, and the slight nudge to her sense of humor was enough to steady her knees, although she continued to regard Langston warily. He was clearly very angry.

"What is wrong, Mr. Langston?"

His features relaxed somewhat, and he stepped forward, stretching up a commanding hand. "What do you think you're doing? Come down from there at once."

Taking his outstretched hand, she descended carefully and explained about the painters, adding that Miss Hutton had asked her to attend to tidying the study, since she hadn't had time to do it herself.

"I see." There was an arrested look in his eye now, as he looked down at her. "I don't suppose she remembered that I gave orders for this room to be left as is."

Kendall cast a dismayed look at the many empty shelves and boxes of books. "No, I suppose she must have forgotten," she said lamely. Then she looked up at him, her eyes still wide. "Oh, Steve, I'm terribly sorry. If you'll let Nelly come back, I'll see that everything is put back, although I'm afraid you'll still have to go through those papers and sort them. But perhaps, since we've gone this far, you ought to speak with Meg first," she added with a more hopeful note. "You might decide to let her go ahead. I promise she doesn't mean to disrupt this room for long."

At first he looked as though he meant to debate the issue, but then he seemed to give himself a shake. "I'll send Nelly back anyway," he muttered. "Silly not to do this room, I suppose, since we're doing the whole house. But there's no need for you to be stacking books. The maids can do it."

"As you like," she replied. "It's nearly time for us to go anyway. But do talk with Meg. She'll understand how you feel about this room, and I think you'll like what she plans to do with it."

With a brief nod of what may or may not have been agreement, he left, and a few moments later Kendall went to tidy herself. Meg could handle him, she thought as she washed her face. It was clear now that they would have to keep an eye on Miss Hutton. Kendall didn't think for a minute that the orders had been forgotten. No doubt, Sylvia had seen a chance to reestablish control and had seized it. Sure that Langston's fiery temper would take over the moment he discovered his study had been tampered with, she had no doubt trusted her own ability to manipulate things from there. At least it hadn't been as bad as it might have been. But it did make things difficult. Kendall still wanted words with him, but with his temper already frayed, she didn't know whether her courage would withstand another confrontation. And she knew perfectly well that if she didn't have it out with him soon, she would never do it.

Stifling a sigh, she went to look for Meg and found her in the living room, having a drink with Langston. Meg seemed to have worked her usual magic, because he was sprawled in a chair, drink in hand, completely relaxed. A decided twinkle lurked in his eye, and Meg grinned at her.

"Sun's definitely over the yardarm," she said. "What will you have? Steve's buying."

He got to his feet. "That I am. What can I fix you? Gin and tonic?"

"Please." He smiled at her, and her heart seemed to flip-flop in her chest. She firmly ordered it to behave itself and turned with outward composure to take her drink from him.

"Meg's explained about the study," he said, "and she's shown me the sketches for a lot of her other ideas. I'm very impressed. Looks as though the results will be terrific."

"Meg's work always looks terrific," Kendall replied loyally, moving toward the sofa and casting an appreciative glance at what was rapidly becoming a classic sunset. There were clouds low on the horizon, and the setting sun shot fire through them, creating a glorious spectacle that was reflected in the sea with breathtaking splendor.

"Beautiful, isn't it?" Langston said quietly, watching her.

She gave him one of her direct, penetrating looks. "Mr. Langston, I'd like to have a word with you, if you don't mind."

"Oops," Meg said, making a comic grimace. "I think that's my cue to make myself scarce for a while. I'll just take my drink out on the patio and watch that gorgeous sunset. And never you mind that I might freeze to death before you two have had it out. I don't mind martyrdom. Not one little bit."

"Don't be silly, Meg," Langston said, smiling at her. "Miss Blake has her jacket, and I am totally immune to the elements. We will go outside, and leave you to enjoy the sunset in comfort. That is, if Miss Blake insists upon a private conversation?"

"I do," Kendall said calmly, ignoring his pointedly formal attitude. "But for your sake, sir, not mine. And there is no need for anyone to go outside. We can discuss this matter just as well in your study."

"What? And miss that sunset? Not on your life, my girl! Besides, you seem to have forgotten that my study is presently uninhabitable. Bring your drink." He held the sliding door open for her, and she went past him and out to a pair of deck chairs poised on the edge of the flagstone patio.

A small wrought-iron and glass table nestled between the two chairs, and Kendall set her drink on it after she had sat down. Langston took the other chair, relaxing completely, his gaze upon the sunset.

Now that the opportunity had come, however, she could not think how to begin. Although she, too, kept her eyes focused upon the brilliant splashes of orange and gold dancing magically on the glassy, rolling sea beyond, she was completely, even physically, aware of the large man sprawled in the chair beside her, and that awareness made it nearly impossible to concentrate upon Mother Nature's spectacular display, let alone upon a properly scathing preamble for the tongue-lashing she yearned to give him.

She bit her lower lip, hoping the small pain would restore her senses to their customary order. It didn't. A brief, sidelong glance revealed a tiny smile tugging at the corners of Langston's lips. She looked quickly back at the ocean. The silence seemed to deepen, but still she could not think how to begin. Words bounced around in her mind, but there was nothing she could bring herself to say aloud to him.

"Well?" he said finally, still without looking at her.

"Why haven't you returned my call?" she blurted. The moment the words were out, she wanted to recall them. She had not sounded annoyed, merely petulant.

"Self-protection," he replied, amused. "I thought it best to give you a chance to become accustomed to all your new little gadgets before we discussed them."

"How dared you order all that done without asking me first!" she demanded. Her voice was low and husky, almost breathless, but she was beginning to regain her emotional feet.

"Because I knew you'd be obstinate about it," he said bluntly, "and every bit of it is necessary for your safety."

"But it will cost a fortune!"

"I never asked you to pay for it."

"But *you* can't!"

"Why not? I want to."

"That's beside the point. It simply isn't done. I hardly know you!"

"We can change that if it's the only thing bothering you," he said quietly. "Is it?"

"No, of course not," Kendall retorted. "It's . . . well, you can't just walk into a person's life and start ordering things to suit yourself. It . . . it turns everything upside down," she ended lamely.

Langston turned his head to look at her. "You're a stubborn lady, Kendall Blake," he said gently, "but I can outstubborn you any day of the week. There's no way I'm going to order those things removed now that they're there, and I sincerely doubt that you'd be idiotic enough to hire someone else to undo the work that's been done."

"No, of course I wouldn't," she muttered. "But that sort of high-handedness makes me absolutely furious."

He grinned at her. "Well, if this is furious, all I can say is that it's not nearly so bad as I was led to expect."

"Don't laugh, damn you. It made me so mad I could cheerfully have strangled you if you'd crossed my path at the time. And what led you to *expect* any particular sort of temperament from me, anyway?"

"Not what," he corrected. "Who. Meg said I'd better polish up every ounce of my famous charm if I meant to survive this confrontation. She warned me in no uncertain terms that you're a real firebrand when you get riled—even said that you bite and scratch and throw things. Didn't believe that last bit myself. You're too self-possessed for such uncivilized fireworks. And I should know, being a past master of the art myself."

"I don't think your fireworks are quite the same," Kendall said musingly. "You seem to blow up over trifles, but then it all goes away. It takes quite a lot to make me angry, but when I lose control, I really lose it. Meg was right to warn you. It's been quite a long time since I last bit anyone—and that was only my brother George, anyway—but I have been known to throw things."

"Wouldn't advise trying it on me," he teased, but with a half-serious glint in his eye. "Could be, I'd take exception to such treatment."

She grinned at him. "I'll bet you would at that."

"That's better," he said approvingly. "Dare I ask now if you still intend to drive down the coast with me tomorrow?"

"There's one thing we need to get clear first."

"What's that?"

"I won't let you pay for any of that equipment. I won't argue the point of necessity any further, but I must insist upon paying for every bit of it myself."

Langston gave her an odd look. "Have you got any idea how much it will cost you?"

"No," she replied stoutly, "but it doesn't matter. I'll pay it."

He shrugged. "Have it your own way. I'll see that you get the bill. Now, will you go with me tomorrow?"

"I should say no," she retorted, but with a gleam of amusement now that she had won her point. "You've been getting your own way far too much for it to be good for you. Being left in the lurch would no doubt be a salutary lesson."

"More than likely I'd throw a temper tantrum instead."

"It really is a pity someone didn't think to smack that inclination out of you when you were a child," she observed cordially.

He chuckled. "It wasn't for lack of trying. I'm just a slow learner. Have you evaded the issue at hand long enough now? Because I'd like an answer to my question if it's all the same to you."

She gave him a direct look. "What time?"

"Elevenish. I've got an early meeting that's likely to drag on a bit, but I couldn't get out of it. After that, the day is ours." He grinned at her, obviously well pleased with himself, and her eyes twinkled in response. The sun had dipped below the horizon at last, and the colors in the sky began to fade. The breeze picked up, and it began to grow noticeably chillier, but they finished their drinks in companionable silence before rejoining Meg in the living room. A few minutes later a phone call from Sylvia Hutton reminded Langston that he had half an hour to get ready for a dinner appointment with some visiting dignitaries. Kendall noted that he said nothing about the mix-up over the study, but he did seem rather abrupt on the phone, and she had the distinct feeling that Miss Hutton would hear his opinion on the subject soon enough. He hung up and apologized for having to cut their cocktail hour short, but Kendall and Meg assured him that it was time for them to go anyway, so he saw them to the door.

Once they were in the car, Meg turned to Kendall. "Well, who won that round?"

"I'm not sure. We both won a point or two, but I've got a very strong notion that he's a shade ahead."

"Tell me." Kendall complied, and Meg let out a low whistle when she learned that Kendall still meant to pay for all the work that had been done at the beachfront house. "How in the world will you be able to afford all *that?*"

Kendall didn't take her eyes from the road, but the worry she had been feeling since she'd won her point with Langston sounded in her voice. "I don't know. It's bound to be expensive, too, but I've got to do it, Meg. I can't be under that sort of obligation to a man like Stephen Langston. You do understand that, don't you?"

"Do you think that's why he did it?" Awe sounded in Meg's clear voice. It was a factor that she obviously hadn't considered before.

Kendall chuckled. "No. To give credit where it's due, I doubt if the notion of using his generosity to press for other, more personal advantages would ever occur to him. In fact, I think if I were to accuse him of such a line of thinking, he'd blow sky-high. He's the sort who sees a problem and does what is necessary to fix it, riding roughshod over anyone who stands in his way, but I'm sure he'd be much more likely to use force of personality than bribery. Besides, I doubt if he thinks any such tactics would be necessary where sex is concerned. He thinks he is irresistible."

"Is he?"

Kendall was silent. The conversation suddenly seemed to be getting beyond her. Headlights of oncoming cars flashed past with more regularity now as they drove into Carmel. She hadn't been driving particularly fast, but she reduced her speed even more, hoping Meg would think she was concentrating on the traffic and not just evading the question. She didn't know how to answer it, because she really hadn't begun to come to terms with her feelings for Langston. Just being in his presence or, for that matter, hearing his voice on the phone did undeniably strange things to her. She responded to him as she had never responded to anyone before. But admitting an attraction for the man was one thing; allowing herself to fall in love was quite another. Besides, he was only interested in her for one reason. He had been perfectly clear about that. He wanted to go to bed with her. Perhaps the relationship might even develop into a full-fledged affair if she were to cooperate. But he had certainly made no noises that sounded remotely like an interest in marriage. He was probably married to his work. Men like Langston often were. It was how they got to the top.

Meg tactfully let the silence lengthen, but when they reached her cottage, she invited Kendall to stay for dinner.

"Not tonight, thanks," Kendall replied, smiling at her. "I've got things to do. Tomorrow is a big day, and I won't have time to do such ordinary things as laundry, ironing, and so forth and so forth."

Meg laughed. "All right, martyr. But don't think you're fooling me for a moment, because you're not. I know you just aren't ready to talk about him, and since I'm the tactful sort, I'll let you off the hook—for the moment, anyway. Have a good time tomorrow!" She waved jauntily and hurried up to the door. Kendall smiled, gave a little shake of her head, then drove on to the beachfront house and parked in the carport. With a small sigh of resignation, she found the key for the gate and got out of the car, pressing down the lock automatically before she shut the door.

Fumbling slightly, she managed to get the gate open and shut again, and it occurred to her for the first time that casual visitors were going to have a slight problem. There was no bell. Since Carmel had no mail delivery, she didn't need to worry about the postman, but how in the world would she ever hear anyone knocking? Not to mention that she would have to come out to the gate to let them in! Something would have to be done about it. Maybe she could hang a bell with a rope that visitors could yank. Oh well, she thought, time enough to think about that little problem later.

The lights were on in the living room when she entered. It really was cozy to come home to a house that seemed to be expecting her. She hung up her jacket and went to see about dinner. Then, with the meal under way, she made a list. Kendall always made lists. They were her way of keeping herself organized. Tonight, she would do her laundry, change the bed, and pamper herself a bit. Tomorrow, she would run the vacuum and dust before Steve came to pick her up. It occurred to her now that she was really looking forward to the trip. No doubt that was merely because it had been years since she had last driven down the coast as far as Big Sur.

Langston arrived punctually at eleven. She had been watching for him, but she made no move toward the gate. Instead, keeping well out of sight, she watched through the front window as he strode up the path to the house. He paused in front of the gate with a look of satisfaction when his eye came to rest upon the shiny brass lock. But the look quickly changed to one of near consternation when he raised his hand to knock. The heavy, rough timber gate simply did not invite one to bang one's tender knuckles upon it. Kendall smiled. Then, taking pity on him, she went out and let him in.

"Good morning," she said cheerfully.

"Good morning, yourself," he grinned, casting an admiring look at her bright yellow skirt and matching sweater. "I see I forgot one small detail. I'll get somebody on it right away. You look absolutely wonderful."

"No, you don't, Mr. Langston!" she declared with amusement. "Thank you for the compliment, but you won't slide that other bit past me so easily. I'm going to hang a brass bell over the gate. Visitors can just yank the rope if they want to come in. You are not going to install any more gadgets, and that's final."

He chuckled. "Okay, okay! Are you ready to go?" She nodded. "Good, then can we declare a truce for the day? I promise I'll behave myself if you will."

"Agreed." She smiled up at him, went to get her purse and jacket, and after carefully locking the gate, they were off.

It was a perfect day for their excursion, she thought, as he drove along the winding beachfront road, then back through town to the Plaza, before following Ocean Avenue up the long, steep hill to the highway. Kendall loved to drive along Highway One because as soon as one left the Peninsula behind the area seemed to be practically unpopulated. They passed the Carmel Valley Road, and she expected Langston to speed up, but he didn't. Instead he continued to drive at a leisurely fifty miles per hour until he slowed considerably and turned off the main road into Point Lobos State Reserve.

"We'll just take things easy," he said as he coasted to a stop at the ranger's booth. He paid the entrance fee and drove on. "I thought we could stop here for a little walk. I love this place."

She agreed, glad she had worn sensible shoes. Though she had slipped a pair of heeled sandals into her tote bag just in case she might need them, she was wearing yellow-and-white rubber-soled sneakers.

They wandered peacefully along the trails, exclaiming over the spectacular views of the sea. The tide was out, and colonies of sea urchins, anemones, starfish, and scuttling hermit crabs provided entertainment for them whenever they bent to examine one of the rocky pools along the shoreline. Kendall's sneakers betrayed her on a particularly slippery rock near one tidepool, and she nearly lost her footing entirely, but a quick, strong hand under her elbow saved her from a wetting, and it seemed only natural after that to acquiesce when he put his arm around her waist.

As they continued their explorations, the sea gulls overhead maintained a constant screech, swooping down and harshly demanding tidbits from tourists who obligingly tossed them scraps of bread and peanuts. Kendall chuckled when a particularly feisty pair of the birds battled in midair over which one had title to a large crust. Finally the crust itself seemed to decide the issue for them, parting in two with a flurry of crumbs.

Steve guided her a little further to a point from which they could see Bird Island, and when they paused to watch the antics of the cormorants and brown pelicans, his arm tightened momentarily. Then it dropped away as he commented that it was a shame it was too late to hope for a glimpse of the California gray whales that travel close to the shoreline from November through January on their annual 12,000-mile migration to Lower California. Conscious of a strong sense of disappointment that he had taken his arm away, Kendall agreed. She enjoyed watching the huge mammals as they humped placidly through the waves, blowing water spouts many feet into the air.

Forty-five minutes after they had left it, they returned to the car, drove out of the reserve and back onto Highway One. Langston rolled his window down a few inches.

"I like fresh air," he said. "Unless you're feeling a draft." She denied it, but he reached behind her to check for himself. As though he believed she might keep any feelings of discomfort to herself, she thought. Just so he could enjoy his fresh air. But instead of irritating her, the gesture brought a little smile to her lips. It was as though he meant to take care of her in spite of herself, and she was beginning to like the notion more and more.

The road began to follow the rugged coastline, clinging precariously to the seaward face of the Santa Lucia Mountains, and providing dramatic bursts of scenery as it twisted, dipped, and rose to thrilling heights. They crossed the spectacular Bixby Creek Bridge, arching 260 feet above the mouth of the tiny creek below, and chuckled together trying to name the many TV commercials and programs that had featured the beautiful structure. Though the road was only two lanes and had narrow shoulders, there were numerous scenic turnouts, and Steve parked the car often so that they could simply drink in the view. Kendall was thoroughly enjoying his company. There were long, comfortable silences punctuated by patches of animated conversation, and—just as they had that night at the Sardine Factory—they seemed to talk about everything and nothing in particular. During one particularly long silent period she let her gaze drift away from the coastal view toward her companion.

In profile he looked even more ruggedly handsome than he did full-face. His chin was sharply etched, which made the stubborn look more noticeable than usual, she thought, suppressing a grin. His nose was straight, his lips even, and his eyes were deeply set under full brows and long, thick lashes. She knew he wouldn't turn toward her because he was the sort of driver who kept his eyes on the road, and he certainly wouldn't change such a habit on a road like this one. Nevertheless, she didn't let her gaze linger. He would notice if she seemed to be staring, and he was just the sort to demand to know what she was thinking. They came to the hairpin curve that marks the mouth of the Little Sur River, and he observed idly that he had always thought he would like to live on the bluff overlooking the southern side of the delta.

Kendall chuckled. "Imagine having to make your way down that cliffside every time you wanted to wander on the beach."

"Make my way, nothing!" he exclaimed with a twinkle. "What's the use of having an army of geniuses at my beck and call if I can't use them for something practical once in a while? I intend to have an elevator that drops right down through that cliffside to the beach. Then, whenever I want to wander, I'll just press B for beach, and there I'll be. My elevator would deposit me in one of those cozy little rock-lined inlets, where the cliffs tower and the waves roar. Very romantic."

"Have you ever been down on that beach?" Kendall asked innocently.

The twinkle in his eyes deepened. "I have."

"Well, so have I, and I nearly got caught by the incoming tide in one of those cozy little inlets you speak of so glibly. It was not romantic at all. As a matter of fact, it was downright terrifying. Besides, your elevator would have to be equipped with waterproof machinery, and more than likely, you'd find the doors opening upon a wall of water instead of a beach. Might come as a bit of a shock when that happened, wouldn't you agree?"

"It might at that," he replied, grinning. "Guess I'll have to contrive something better before I build my house."

Silence descended again, and Kendall allowed herself to drift back to her reveries. It was amazing to her that she could feel so much at home with Langston, that one moment he could infuriate her and the next seem to be such a very old friend. What on earth, she wondered, was she getting herself into? She must not allow herself to be lured into caring too much for this man. To do so could only lead to heartache.

Suddenly, Langston braked and swung the car sharply to the right. Grabbing the dashboard for support, Kendall gasped with dismay, for they had come around a tall, broken dome of black rock and now seemed to be plunging straight off the high, craggy cliff into open space. Then she realized that there was, in fact, still a road under them, and she let out a slow breath of relief as her hand dropped back to her lap.

"Almost missed it," Langston said with a touch of amusement that told her he had noted her reaction. "Sorry if I startled you."

"Where are we going?"

"Rocky Point Lodge. I'm starving."

"Seems to me you're always starving."

"Fact of life," he grinned. "I've got a lot to keep up, you know."

"True," she agreed. "But I'll confess I'm hungry, too."

The cliff-perched lodge served a very fine lunch, and they lingered over it, enjoying the view. It was the same coastline and the same blue Pacific they had been watching all the way from Point Lobos; yet, Kendall thought fondly, she never grew tired of it. It was like watching a living, breathing creature pounding away at obstinate rock monsters. Her gaze encountered her companion's, and the expression she saw in his eyes told her that his feelings for the sea were as strong as her own. The thought was like a warm blanket.

After lunch, they continued down the coast past the Point Sur lighthouse, standing out on the headland like a huge stone spike. There was no activity now, with the bright sun shining, but Kendall knew that at night and on foggy days, the lighthouse flashed a warning every fifteen seconds that could be seen as much as twenty-five miles out to sea. She settled back comfortably, letting her thoughts wander where they would, nearly mesmerized by the beauty of the passing coastline.

CHAPTER 7

Not long afterward they passed Andrew Molera State Park, a primitive area encompassing the lower section of the Big Sur River, which has been permanently closed to motorized vehicles. Moments later they drove into Big Sur. The little village hugging the boundaries of Los Padres National Forest and the notoriously rugged Ventana wilderness area had been a haunt of hippies and tourists for so long that it was refreshing to note as Steve parked the car that the area was, for once, almost barren of people.

They wandered through various shops and galleries without buying anything, then strolled beneath the giant redwood trees of the park itself and down onto the beach. Once there they pulled off their shoes, then meandered along the shoreline, scuffing their feet through the sand and drawing ridiculous pictures with their toes just so they could watch the breakers wash the drawings away again. The sun had dipped much lower, and Kendall realized suddenly that a slight haze seemed to have developed on the horizon. Steve followed her gaze, and his forehead knitted into a frown.

"We'll have to keep an eye on that."

"Fog, do you think?"

"Probably, but whether its going to develop into a pea souper or stay civilly offshore, I can't say." He glanced down at her. "It's beginning to be a bit chilly down here. Do you want to go back to the car?"

"Whenever you say," she replied demurely, staring at her bare toes as they wiggled in the damp sand.

"How refreshing," he observed in a low voice, watching

her closely. "You're actually going to let me start calling the tune?"

"I didn't say that." She looked up at him, and her breath nearly caught in her throat at the expression in his eyes. Steve tossed his shoes carelessly to the sand, then rested his hands gently upon her shoulders.

"There is something I have been wanting to do ever since I arrived at your house this morning, sweet Kendall Blake, but I've been afraid you'd plunge me into the deep freeze if I tried it." He hesitated, but she said nothing at all, nor did she unlock her gaze from his. Slowly, he drew her close, lowered his head, and kissed her gently. Then he straightened, held her away, and looked down into her eyes again. "Well?"

His eyes seemed to smolder, and he held her gaze. Kendall opened her mouth to speak, but no words came. It was as though she were hypnotized. Her body seemed to move toward his of its own accord, and before she knew what had happened, his arms were around her again, and she was losing herself in a kiss that had started just as gently as its predecessor. But something seemed to stir within her, a tiny spark that kindled deep down inside, then flamed into something that sent burning tremors throughout her body. Kendall had read about soul-stirring kisses, but the term had always seemed fanciful, a product of a romantic author's imagination. Now she wasn't so sure.

Don't be ridiculous, girl, said her better self as the yellow-and-white sneakers slipped unnoticed from Kendall's grasp. It's nothing so innocent as your soul being stirred. It's much more down-to-earth than that. Tell him he's got to behave himself!

His hand slipped under her jacket to move in a feather-light caress over her breast, and the tingles that went through her at his touch effectively silenced her better self. She melted toward him, feeling warm and feminine and perfectly at home in his strong embrace.

"Hi, guys!"

At the sound of the high-pitched, adenoidal voice, Kendall

stiffened. She opened her eyes to meet Steve's twinkling gaze. With one accord, they looked down at the source of the greeting, a small, wire-haired boy with about six years of life's experiences behind him, holding up a handful of mostly broken seashells for their inspection.

"Hi, yourself," said Langston. "Who are you?"

"Jimmy. See my shells?"

"They're beautiful," Kendall said with just the right touch of admiration to bring a proud smile to his face. "But aren't you a bit young to be out here by yourself?"

"Not by myself," he said sturdily. "With my daddy and *her.*" He wrinkled his nose disdainfully and pointed down the beach. A man in cutoff Levis and a T-shirt, and a young barely-bikini-clad woman were slowly approaching them, their arms intimately intwined, their hands roaming, as they gazed soulfully into one another's eyes. "She's *not* my mommy."

"Oh," said Kendall, carefully avoiding Steve's eye. "But you've got a lot of shells, haven't you."

"Yup," replied the tot, regarding her with speculation. "You're very pretty. D'ya know if they got the kind of shells down here you can hear the ocean in?"

Kendall smiled at him but shook her head. "They have some in the shops, but I doubt if you'll find any like that just lying about on the beach. Only the sort you've found already."

"It wouldn't hurt to look though," Steve pointed out, adding quickly, "But we can't help you. We've got to go now." He put his arm firmly around Kendall's shoulders, snatched up their shoes, and guided her back toward the car. "They didn't look as though they'd appreciate our company," he muttered when they were out of earshot, "and I know I wouldn't have appreciated theirs."

When they got back to the car, he informed her that he had made reservations for dinner at Nepenthe, the famous restaurant some three miles south of Pfeiffer-Big Sur State Park. "You can't be starving again already," she teased him.

"Nope," he agreed with a chuckle, "but if we hustle a bit we can watch the sunset with our first drink."

Kendall changed her shoes, and by the time they reached Nepenthe, she had also refreshed her lipstick and combed her hair. The big redwood pavilion, designed by a student of the great Frank Lloyd Wright, perched upon a precipice some 800 feet above the sea, so once they had been shown to a table near the window in the cocktail lounge, they were afforded a suitably spectacular view of the setting sun. A pretty waitress approached, and Langston ordered their drinks.

"By the way," he added as the girl turned away, "the name is Langston, and I've got reservations for two to dine at six."

"Certainly, sir," she replied. "I'll inform the maître d' that you can be found in here, shall I?"

"Please." The girl disappeared, and Langston turned back to Kendall, his eyes warm with the pleasure of looking at her. She was staring out the window, in deep contemplation of the view. The glow of the setting sun gilded her complexion and sent highlights dancing through her hair. "Lovely, isn't it?" he said gently. "Did you know this place is built around a honeymoon cottage?"

"Some honeymoon cottage!" she replied, turning to smile at him. "I did hear once that there was a movie star connected with the place. But I forget who it was."

"Rita Hayworth," he replied promptly. "That so-called cottage was built for her in the forties by Orson Welles."

"Orson Welles and Rita Hayworth? Who'd have thunk it? I knew about her brief marriage to the Ali Khan, of course, but I never knew she'd been married to Orson Welles."

"They were quite a pair, I understand. She was incredibly beautiful, of course, and you've got to admit they both had a lot of style."

"And good taste in locations for houses," Kendall replied with twinkling understatement.

"Unlike mine?" he teased.

"I never said your *location* was a bad idea, just your elevator," she murmured. They had been looking into each other's eyes, and she was suddenly deeply conscious of the stirring passions just beneath the surface of his steady gaze. The sun, radiant in pinks and reds and violets, began to slip beneath the horizon unnoticed by either of them.

"I have quite a lot of good ideas, actually," said Langston quietly, his eyes not leaving hers.

"I don't doubt it." Her voice was low.

"Sir? Mr. Langston?"

The cocktail waitress hovered over them, and she had brought more than their drinks. She handed Langston a note. "An urgent message from your office, sir. The maître d' said to bring it immediately. It was phoned through about twenty minutes ago."

Kendall watched curiously while Steve scanned the note. He looked up with a rueful smile. "It's from Sylvia. I've got to call in. Will you excuse me?"

She nodded, taking a sip from her drink and suppressing sudden feelings of outrage as she watched him stride across the room. How did Sylvia Hutton know to find him here? Had he told her their plans for the day? Surely not. But how else would she know to leave a message here? Perhaps he always brought his dates to Nepenthe for dinner. Perhaps she had called every restaurant from Carmel south to leave the same message. But niggling away in the back of Kendall's mind was the thought that he must have told Sylvia where to find him. In his business, emergencies must be almost commonplace, she reflected moodily. Naturally, his office would have to know where to reach him. So why did it annoy her so much that it was Sylvia Hutton who had called him?

Admit it, girl, she thought ruefully. You're jealous of Sylvia Hutton, and undoubtedly without any cause whatsoever. She is merely his executive assistant, nothing more. An ambitious lady, perhaps, but certainly not one for whom the man shows any yen. And that ought to be the key, oughtn't it? It doesn't matter whether Sylvia is interested in him or not. Not if he's not interested in her. And Sylvia isn't interested either, she mused. She doesn't cling on his arm or bat her lashes at him or even seem particularly possessive of the man. So why does the very mention of her name set your hackles rising? Then she remembered the incident concerning the study and frowned. Could Sylvia's contriving possibly have been the act of a jealous woman or was it simply a cattish attempt to get even with Kendall for getting her own way over the color schemes? The latter possibility seemed more than likely. If Sylvia was possessive of anything, she was possessive about her position as Langston's executive assistant.

She had little time to consider the matter any further, however, for the call did not take Steve long to make, and soon he was striding back toward her, a heavy frown on his face. Although he smiled apologetically as he reached the table, he did not sit down. "Drink up, sweetheart," he said gently, laying some bills on the table. "No dinner at Nepenthe after all. I've got to get back right away."

Making a strong effort to conceal her disappointment, Kendall set her glass down with exaggerated care and picked up her purse. "What happened?"

"Can't tell you exactly. Only that some bad men seem to have interested themselves in one of our projects—one I've got a particular interest in, as it happens."

"You mean someone tried to steal classified information?"

"Something like that," he admitted. "Ready?"

She nodded and he helped her put her jacket on. Less than five minutes later, they were on their way. This time, however, it was no leisurely drive. Langston drove as fast as he dared, and Kendall was treated to a display of true skill behind the wheel. It was not, in fact, until she chanced to glimpse the speedometer that she realized how rapidly they were traveling, because his expertise was such that the car slipped through curves and sped along straightaways as though it were attached to some sort of a track, smoothly, effortlessly.

"At least, this way we don't need to worry about being caught in the fog," he commented.

"No," she agreed. Then, "How did Miss Hutton know where to find you?"

There was a small but weighty silence during which Kendall wished she had not spoken, then Steve said quietly, "I gave her a probable itinerary for the day. Even when I declare a holiday, someone has to know where I am. Do you mind?"

"Of course not," she replied with a barely suppressed sigh. "I just wondered." But her studied calm didn't fool him this time.

"She no doubt left word at the Ventana, Big Sur Lodge, the Highlands Inn, Rocky Point, and probably several other places as well," he explained, grinning. "She knows me. I do sometimes change my mind at the last moment, but I trust to her resourcefulness if something goes wrong. Sylvia's resourcefulness can be practically awe-inspiring. However," he added more seriously, "she does tend to get a trifle out of hand upon occasion, and my faith in her resourcefulness doesn't alter the fact that she has managed to annoy me considerably from time to time."

"Oh?" She didn't know what else to say. They had come up behind another car, and Langston was compelled to slow down. She could sense his impatience. It seemed to set the very molecules of air inside the small car dancing with energized tension. Then suddenly, he gave a rueful sigh and relaxed, loosening his grip upon the wheel and stretching the fingers of first one hand, then the other.

"No sense getting riled at a Sunday driver. He'll probably turn off in a minute anyway. She engineered that little mix-up purposely, you know."

Kendall had no trouble following his train of thought. "I was pretty sure that must have been the case. As a matter of fact, the thought crossed my mind the moment I saw you standing in the doorway. You looked positively livid, and I couldn't think of any other reason for it. Poor Nelly!"

Langston chuckled. "There's one who will never get used to my temper."

"People shouldn't have to get used to it," Kendall reproved sternly. "You should learn to control it better, to behave in a more civilized fashion."

"Nonsense. That's how men like me get ulcers. I never will. There's not a bottled-up thought in my body." He paused, then added a bit too casually, "I had a little chat with her this morning."

"A little chat?" Amusement crept into her voice.

"Well, maybe that's just a tad understated. I chewed her out royally, and if her ears aren't still burning, it's no fault of mine. Just thought you deserved to know."

"Why on earth did she do it?" Kendall asked, wondering if he could shed light on that rather perplexing question.

"Sylvia was born to be master of all she surveys," Steve replied matter-of-factly. "If she had been born a male, she would no doubt own one of Langston's competitors by now. As it is, she does her best to run Langston and anything else she chances to hook into. But she likes to be appreciated, too, and she furiously resents the slightest hint of interference from anyone but me. So when I curbed her powers in the Sandcastle project, I'm afraid she blamed you and took umbrage."

"Took it out on Meg and me, you mean," Kendall said, putting the matter into simpler terms. "How could she possibly expect to get away with it?"

In the gathering darkness, she sensed rather than saw his rueful shrug. "I can't say for sure, of course, but I'm afraid she thought my temper would carry the day and I'd let fly at the first person I laid eyes on. It's happened before. Then I guess she expected she'd be able to stage-manage the situation from there." He paused for a moment reflectively before continuing. "I've noticed before that Sylvia's a bit leery of my rages, and she's darn good at her job, so I tend to treat her a little more gently than some of the others I work with. But I couldn't let her get away with that stunt she pulled yesterday. The thing that really bugs me is that she might very well have pulled it off if you weren't so damned good at dashing ice water on my flights of temper."

"Do I do that?"

"You do." He reached over and patted her knee, then let his hand rest there. "Never knew such a wench for stifling temper tantrums. One look into your frosty eyes, and I feel about two feet tall—and two years old," he added ruefully.

Kendall chuckled, and with a gentle, parting squeeze of her knee, Steve returned his hand to the steering wheel and soon changed the subject. A few moments later the car in front of them obligingly pulled off the road onto one of the viewing turnouts, so he was able to increase their speed again. The trip back to Carmel took just over half an hour to accomplish after that, and they were soon pulling up in front of Kendall's house. Steve jumped out and hurried around to help her from the car. "Sorry about dinner," he said, but then he paused as a thought struck him. "Look here, I doubt if this matter will actually take me more than an hour or so to clear up. What would you say to a late supper somewhere here in town or over on the wharf?"

"Sounds fine," she said, absurdly delighted that their day would not come to quite such a blunt ending. "But why not just stay here when you get back? I could fix us a light supper."

"Gee, can you cook, too?" he asked, wide-eyed.

"Fool," she replied, handing him the gate key. "I am a very good cook, and I'd like to do it." They passed through the gate to the front door, and Langston inserted the key before he replied.

"A supper here with you sounds terrific," he said quietly, looking down at her, his eyes beginning to smolder again. She turned to him naturally, and the key was left to dangle in the lock. He kissed her lightly, then held her close and kissed her again. This time the burning sensation seemed to curl her toes and work its way up from there. When he finally relaxed his hold, Kendall was surprised to discover that she could still breathe. "Tell me something," he murmured close to her hair.

"What?" Her own voice was breathless, nearly a whisper.

"How long and how well do you have to know me before you'll let me take you to bed?"

Kendall stiffened, moving away from him with careful dignity. "This may come as a real shock to you, Steve," she said, anger tingeing words that came without thought, "but I have no intention of setting up a production schedule for you. Today has been wonderful, and I *was* looking forward to your company later, but you will not be welcome if your only reason in coming is to entice me to go to bed with you. Do I make myself clear?"

"Perfectly." He regarded her with speculatively narrowed eyes. "I believe you mean it, too," he said slowly. "Does this mean supper is off?"

"Not if you still want to come and will agree to respect my feelings in this matter."

"I still want to," he replied, looking down at her. "I didn't mean to upset you. It's just that I dislike game-playing. When I want something I ask for it. It usually gets results quicker than any tactful beating about the bush, but I'll admit this isn't the first time I've stuck my foot in my mouth. Sorry if I've offended you."

"Fair enough, as you like to say. How soon do you expect to get back?"

"I can't say for certain. Will it matter?"

"No, I've got any number of things I can whip up at the drop of a hat. I'll just wait for the patter of your little feet before I actually start cooking."

"Your efficiency fills me with admiration," he chuckled, but she noted the relief in his voice. "Come along now, and lock the gate behind me. I'll finish this business as quickly as I can." He made no attempt to kiss her again, but before he disappeared through the gate, he squeezed her hand and grinned reassuringly down at her. Warmed by the gesture, Kendall hurriedly locked the gate and strode back into the house to examine her larder. She couldn't remember what she had, but she was almost certain she would have to go to the store. What on earth had possessed her to invite him back for supper? No wonder the man had gotten ideas! And why had she answered him the way she had? She had certainly never meant to take such a hard-bitten stand. Now he probably took her for a prim and proper virgin, which was not what she had intended at all. She actually considered herself to be rather liberal-minded, but since he had walked into her life, she just didn't seem to know her own mind anymore. She responded to his advances as though she was leading him on to grander, more glorious things, but when he moved to take advantage of her seemingly relaxed attitude, something inside just rebelled. She reacted without conscious thought. Perhaps it was simply that that better self of hers resented the fact that Steve Langston seemed interested only in how quickly he could maneuver her into bed. She sighed, forcing her thoughts back to supper.

Since she usually did her grocery shopping on Saturday, the cupboards were practically bare, so out came the paper and pencil. She decided the easiest thing would be to make clam chowder. She knew Langston liked Boston style, because they had ordered it at the Sardine Factory, and she made excellent chowder herself. With French bread and salad, it would make a very good supper, and maybe one of the bakeries would still be open and she could get something gooey for dessert. With her list made, she hurried out to her car and went first to the bakery, knowing that if it was still open, it wouldn't be for much longer. Luckily, her favorite bakery still showed a light in the window, and she was able to purchase a loaf of sourdough French bread as well as a delicious-looking cherry pie. Dashing from bakery to grocery store, she made her purchases, adding vanilla ice cream to the list in case Steve liked his pie à la mode, and then drove quickly back to the beachfront.

As she pulled into the carport, she noticed that there seemed to be more cars than usual parked along the street.

But it was, after all, Saturday night, and young people still thought walking on the beach a romantic pastime, so she thought little about it. Deciding to come back for the pie, she unloaded her two bags of groceries and, walking quickly over the familiar ground despite the darkness, made her way up to the gate. She set down her grocery bags in order to find the gate key, and suddenly a car door opened across the street, and a familiar voice shouted at her.

"Hey, babe, wait a minute!" A tall, lanky figure began to jog toward her, but before he could get halfway across the street, headlights flashed up on two other cars, followed by shouts and the sound of running feet. The man in the street paused, then yelled in protest as two burly figures descended on him.

Kendall stared in astonishment for some moments before she recollected herself. "Stop that!" she shouted then. "Leave him alone, or I'll call the police!" She started to unlock the gate, then seeing another car approaching, decided to try for help nearer at hand. Running toward the street, she waved frantically, her gestures clear in the light from the many headlamps. But the car passed right by, ignoring the tableau in the street and, if anything, speeding up rather than slowing down. Catching a brief but clear glimpse of two men inside, Kendall gave a *humph* of disgust and whirled back toward the house.

"Wait, Miss Blake! It's all right. We've got him! It's perfectly safe now."

More astonished than ever, Kendall turned abruptly to see one of the attackers waving at her. The man who had first called out to her had his hands behind him and was being frog-marched toward one of the lighted cars. The one who had waved began to walk toward her. "Who are you?" she demanded angrily.

"Severson, ma'am," he replied. "Langston Industries security." He reached into an inside jacket pocket and extracted a leather case. Flipping it open, he displayed an identity card.

"Langston! He sent you here?"

"Yes, ma'am. We've been watching your house all week. Guess this is just the sort of thing he musta been expecting, but we got our man all right."

"Mr. Severson," Kendall said coldly, "the man you *attacked* is a very good friend of mine, and if you do not release him immediately, I shall call the police and have you both charged with assault. How would you and your friend like to explain that to your precious Mr. Langston?"

Even in the dim light, she could see that Severson had lost color. He mumbled something, then cleared his throat and squared his shoulders. "I'm right sorry if we've made an error, ma'am, but it was perfectly natural after everything else that's happened today—the way that fellow jumped out of his car and shouted at you. Then he started running toward you and . . . well, I'm sure Mr. Langston would understand the error." But his voice trailed off doubtfully on the final words.

Under any other circumstance Kendall might have felt a twinge of pity for him, but she was furious, and it was with icy rage that she demanded that the men release Jack at once. They obeyed, and Jack gave his wholehearted support to her command that they leave immediately and never return. But this Severson could not agree to do.

"I'm really sorry to have upset you, Miss Blake, but I'm sure you must understand that we can't desert our post without direct orders from Mr. Langston himself."

"Then I'll see that you get them before the night is out," Kendall promised frostily, pointedly turning her back on the man as she twisted her key in the gate lock. She stooped to pick up her groceries and went into the house, followed by a bewildered Jack. "I apologize for that," she said to him once they were inside.

"What happened?" he asked, rubbing his head. He was tall and lanky with light brown eyes and fine, straight blond hair that had a tendency to fall over his eyes. She explained, and he frowned disapprovingly. "Who does this guy think he is, anyway? I just came over to find out why you've been avoiding me, and I get jumped by a couple of gun-toting goons. Why in blazes does he think you need armed protection?"

"Stephen Langston doesn't think," Kendall retorted bitterly, moving toward the kitchen. "He just does things. He decided that this house is a prowler trap, and he doesn't trust me—a mere female, after all—to take care of myself, so he does it for me. But he's gone too far this time." She set her groceries down with a thump on the table.

"What do you mean, 'this time?' What else has he done?" She hesitated, and he growled, "Come on, babe, tell me. This is making me crazy."

So she told him about the locks and the lighting, but in the telling, she found herself defending Langston's actions, making light of them, rationalizing the necessity for each piece of new equipment. Jack's eyes narrowed more and more with each word, and by the time she finished, he was glaring at her.

"And just what does your infernal Mr. Langston expect to get in return for all his electronic wizardry? Or has he already collected?" he asked sarcastically.

"How dare you say such a thing, Jack Susmann!" Kendall flashed. "If you think for one moment that I would allow—"

"Who knows what you'd allow a guy with that kind of power and money!" he snapped, his anger as great as her own. "By God, Kendall, you've been seeing him all week. You won't even talk to me, and I thought we had a pretty good thing going. I sure as check have a right to know what's been going on behind my back!"

"Nothing has been going on," she returned, weariness replacing anger, "and certainly not behind your back. You and I don't have any sort of understanding between us, Jack, and most assuredly not the sort that would make me answerable in any way to you for my actions!"

"Well, maybe we don't have one yet," he admitted, sulking, "but I sure thought it was headed that way."

"It wasn't," she retorted flatly. "We have been friends, that's all. And I think it would be very wise if you were to leave now and not call me for a while. The gate's still un-locked. You can see yourself out."

He looked at her in protest, but she met that look, and her eyes were set hard. He shrugged. "Whatever you say, babe. But don't hold your breath expecting that call." With that Parthian shot, he turned away, and a moment later she heard the front door snap shut behind him.

"Men!" she exclaimed, snatching groceries from the bag and banging them down on the table. She knew Jack would call again once he calmed down, but she didn't really care whether he did or not. Her world did not revolve around Jack Susmann. And Langston had definitely overstepped himself this time! How dared he set men to watch her! To think that they had been out there every night this week, watching her every move. The impudence! The outrageous arrogance of the man. Without telling her a word about it, too. Leaving her to be frightened half to death by a scene such as the one that had just taken place. It was too much. When she got finished with Mr. Langston, he would be sorry he'd ever conceived such a notion.

CHAPTER 8

Kendall finished putting the groceries away, entertaining herself with visions of Langston in thumbscrews, on the rack, the wheel—and what exactly was an iron maiden? Sounded too good for him, whatever it was. It sounded distinctly female, which fact alone ought to make it an appropriate device for his punishment, but he'd probably just charm it into taking a number behind the rest of his *ladies*. Even that absurd twist of thought failed to make her smile. With brisk efficiency, she rinsed the lettuce and put it in the crisper, peeled her potatoes, sautéed the onions and bacon, added the water and clam juice, then put the potatoes in to boil.

It didn't occur to her that there was anything the least bit incongruous in her activities. She had promised him supper, so supper would be provided. But she meant to snatch the man bald-headed before he had so much as taken a single bite!

Once the potatoes had come to a boil, she turned down the gas and went in to take a quick shower and change her clothes. Fifteen minutes later, she was back at the stove, glowing from the shower and smelling of fresh cologne, the yellow outfit replaced by gray wool slacks and a tailored paisley shirt. She poked the potatoes with a fork and decided they were ready, so she added her cream and clams, a tablespoon of butter, salt and pepper, and the dash of instant mashed potatoes that was her secret ingredient, giving the chowder its perfect consistency. Then, turning the gas as low as it would go, she covered the pot and left things to simmer lightly while she set the table.

A moment later, she stepped back to inspect the results.

Bright yellow place mats and fringed napkins rested upon a yellow-and-white checked cloth. The dark brown crockery soup tureen had been filled with hot water, and the silverware, water glasses, and bread and butter were in place. All that remained was to put the dishes on the table. She turned to the cupboard and selected bread plates, salad plates, and two of her big, flat-rimmed soup bowls. She placed the smaller dishes first, and was just putting the first soup bowl down when she was startled by the sound of the front door banging open, followed by rapid-fire footsteps in the hall behind her.

"Kendall! What the devil do you mean by leaving that gate wide open and the front door unlocked! Are you out of your ever-loving mind, girl?"

She whirled to find Langston looming in the doorway, his face black with worry-turned-to-anger; and, without so much as a fleeting thought for the wisdom of her action, she launched the remaining soup bowl at him with as much strength as she could muster. Startled, he caught it, looking down at it as though he couldn't quite believe that she had thrown it; then, he looked up again—and laughed.

"For Pete's sake, Meg was right!" he chortled. "But I never thought you would. Never!"

Kendall advanced upon him, eyes blazing with wrath. "How dare you laugh at me, Stephen Langston! How dare you set your imbecilic little Keystone Cops to spy upon me! You are far and away the most contemptible, arrogant, overbearing man I've ever met. Do you even know what happened here tonight? Have you got any idea how ridiculous I felt trying to explain that imbroglio to Jack? He would be perfectly within his rights if he decided to call the police and press charges of assault against your two dunderheaded watchdogs! And you're worse than they are—thinking you can do just as you please without so much as a by-your-leave from anyone. But I'll have you know that I, for one, won't stand for it!"

"Whoa there, sweetheart, and let me get a word in."

"I am *not* your sweetheart, and I cannot imagine a single word you might say that I should be at all interested to hear. And don't touch me!" she snapped, when he reached toward her.

His own anger flared again. "I *should* touch you," he retorted with grim meaning. "And you're going to listen to me. No, you don't!" he added sharply, reaching to stop her when she began, angrily, to turn away from him. But at the touch of his hand on her arm, Kendall whirled on him furiously, and her hand flew up to strike. He caught her wrist easily, but she had now lost her temper completely and swung at him wildly with the other hand. Somehow, he caught that wrist, too, and it was the final straw.

"Let me go, damn you!" she shouted at him, wrenching herself first one way, then another, and kicking angrily at his legs in an effort to free herself from that iron grip. For a bare second, it seemed that he had released her, and she began to fall away from him, only to be stopped when the same hands that had already bruised her wrists clamped down painfully upon her shoulders. She began to struggle again, but her efforts seemed useless. He was shouting at her, but she couldn't hear what he was saying. It was as though she were someone else watching a scene with no sound, someone who had no control over any of the action. Then suddenly he was shaking her, and she had no control over anything. It felt as though her head would fly off, and she couldn't breathe properly. The shaking stopped finally, but his fingers still dug sharply into her shoulders.

"Now you listen to me, and you listen good," he ordered coldly, giving her another, much lighter shake. She stared at him. The ice in his voice went right through her, sending flying chills up and down her spine, turning her knees to quivering jello. This was not his usual temper flaring. This was much, much worse. It frightened her. She had no idea what he might do to her, but she knew instinctively that she had better tread with a very light step. White-faced, she swallowed carefully, not taking her eyes from his. "I put those men out there for your safety," he went on in the same frostbitten tone, "and not for any other reason. I didn't tell you about them because I thought it would make you uncomfortable to know they were there. I'm sorry about the mix-up with your friend, but you might consider how different it would have been if he had been someone else. Someone with less pleasant intentions toward you. It's entirely possible, you know."

"I *don't* know," Kendall replied weakly, striving to regain her composure and failing miserably. She couldn't remember the last time anyone had even come close to reducing her to tears, but she knew that if something didn't happen to prevent it, she would soon be sobbing her eyes out. "I got along well enough before I met you, and I can think of no reason that I should suddenly be in danger now," she muttered helplessly.

The grip on her shoulders relaxed slightly. "Nevertheless, you are," he said. "I'm not just a pushy so-and-so, you know. There are reasons for my actions. You have been in danger ever since you came into my life."

"But Meg came into your life, too, and you haven't forced any of this stuff on her," Kendall protested.

"There are men watching Meg, too," he said simply.

Kendall's eyes widened. She straightened, gathering dignity again. "I think," she said carefully, "that there is a bit more to all this than you have told me."

"Yes."

She remembered what he had told her about the classified projects he was involved with. *"Can* you tell me?"

"I can tell you enough," he replied, watching her. "Are you all right now?" She nodded meekly. It had been a long, long time since she had lost her temper so completely with anyone, and she was feeling slightly ashamed of herself. Langston seemed to realize it. He smiled, gave her a little hug, and nudged her toward the table. "Why don't we sit down."

She nodded again and moved obediently toward her chair, grateful that her legs didn't fail her. She felt completely

wrung out. Langston pulled the chair out for her and took the
one opposite for himself.

"I should have told you before," he said gently, "but I was
afraid it would frighten you. Besides, we didn't know exactly
what we were up against until today."

"So the emergency was a real one." She was regaining her
composure as a result of his quiet manner, and she could
meet his gaze once more.

"If that means you suspected Sylvia of overplaying her
hand again," he said with a chuckle, "I'll admit you might
have had cause. It's even possible that I might have suspected the same thing myself on any other occasion. But
you've forgotten one tiny detail. After this morning's little
chat, she wouldn't have dared try one of her little power
plays."

Kendall looked down at the yellow place mat with a small
shiver. She had forgotten about that so-called little chat, but
if Sylvia had been subjected to a display like the one she had
just seen . . . well, maybe it was possible to feel sympathy
even for someone like Sylvia Hutton.

"The situation was perfectly legitimate," he went on.
"Someone has been trying for some time now to steal the
plans for my pet project, and today they nearly were caught.
As a matter of fact, they tried to kidnap Jerry, but they blew
it."

"What! You mean Russians, or . . . or . . . just who in the
world do you mean?"

"Not Russians," he said with a grin. "Though I don't doubt
that they would be as interested in this information as anyone
else. They are very likely to be one of the bidders if these
guys ever manage to hold an auction. But the would-be
thieves are just as much Yankees as you and I are. Only of a
slightly different breed, I assure you—the sort that doesn't
see anything wrong with selling whatever they can get to the
highest bidder."

"Well, I still don't see how I come into it," Kendall said.

"It's hard enough to imagine that sort of thing going on right here on the Peninsula without being mixed up in it myself."

"Most likely you never will be," he replied easily. "It's just that I don't like to take chances. You never know what monkey business these guys will get up to, and they might think you could be used as leverage to bring me to my senses." She was silent for a moment, digesting his words. Then suddenly he sniffed the air appreciatively. "Do I smell clam chowder?"

Smiling slightly, she nodded. Then, realizing from the not so subtle hint that he must be starving again, she got quickly to her feet and moved toward the stove to stir the chowder. It smelled delicious. She got out the lettuce and mixed a quick salad, then emptied the soup tureen, now barely luke warm, and refilled it with chowder. It wasn't until she set it on the table that she realized something was missing.

"What did you do with the other soup bowl?" she asked with a self-conscious smile.

"On the refrigerator," he replied, grinning back at her. The refrigerator stood next to the door, and she realized he simply must have set the bowl down upon the nearest flat surface when she had tried to slap him. She retrieved it and put it in its place, then ladled chowder into each bowl.

"Are there really men watching Meg?" she asked.

"There are. Do you think we ought to tell her?"

"That depends upon how good they are," Kendall replied with a sweet smile. "Two of her brothers are ex-college linebackers, one from Stanford and the other from UCLA. If they catch your little spies at work, they're likely to make chopped liver out of them first and ask any pertinent questions afterward, assuming anyone is still capable of answering by then. But if your men are really good—"

"They are, but your point is well taken," he said with a mocking grimace. "I think we'll explain this business to Meg."

"Whatever you think best, sir," she replied demurely. Steve laughed.

Their meal proceeded very pleasantly after that, and when

Kendall remembered that she had left the pie in the car, he went obligingly to fetch it for her, noting that they still hadn't locked the gate. He attended to it, and they took their dessert into the living room and opened the drapes to watch the moonlight on the incoming breakers while they gorged themselves on cherry pie à la mode. Then, at his suggestion, Kendall put a Glen Yarborough record on the record player and went back to join him on the sofa. Steve moved to pull her into his arms, but she hesitated, her eyes questioning his intent.

Looking straight back at her, he said gently, "Trust me," and abandoning reasonable thought, Kendall melted into his arms and turned her face up to receive his kisses. He was gentle, and he was tender, and he made no attempt to push her beyond what he had been led to expect that she would tolerate. But his lightest touch sent waves of ecstasy pulsing through her, and she began to think she had been crazy to deny him anything. After a time, she realized that if he were to sweep her into his arms and carry her into the bedroom, she would not deny him. She tried to tell herself that she was glad she could trust him better than she could trust herself. It was true. The knowledge that he was as good as his word gave her a pleasant sense of security that made her increasingly content to be in his company. Nevertheless . . .

It was late when Steve finally took his leave. Kendall followed him out to the gate, and before he opened it he leaned down to kiss her gently on the lips. Then, after a brief hug, he was gone, and with a small sigh of disappointment, Kendall watched him drive away.

A fine thing, girl! scolded her better self sternly. He lets you have your own way, and you're upset about it. A fine, upstanding young woman you are!

Kendall shook herself and decided that all things considered—her temper, her better self, and the bodyguards notwithstanding—the day had turned out much more satisfactorily than it deserved.

The next morning while she was indulging herself in a

leisurely, late breakfast, Steve called from his office to break the news that he would have to fly to San Francisco that evening for a meeting early Monday morning.

"I might have to stay in the city for a couple of days," he added, "but I was hoping you might have enough energy left over from yesterday to join me for a picnic at the beach this afternoon."

Delighted, Kendall agreed with enthusiasm. "What would you like to eat?" she asked.

"Never mind that," he chuckled. "I'll take care of it and pick you up about one, if that's all right with you."

He was there on the dot of one o'clock, and as he helped her into the car, the delicious smell of spicy salami wafted to greet her. "Smells good," she approved when he climbed in beside her. He was wearing Levis and a smoky blue turtleneck, and she thought he needed only a navy peacoat to resemble a sailor home from the sea.

Steve grinned at her. "From my favorite deli," he said. "French sandwich rolls—custom-sliced, of course—salami, various cheeses, apples, and a bottle of wine. Did I forget anything?"

"Only dessert," she teased.

"Hope you like chocolate eclairs."

"Good Lord, Steve! This isn't a picnic, it's a gluttonous orgy!"

Correctly interpreting her exclamation as a stamp of approval, he grinned again, and they were off. She wasn't surprised when he headed toward Pebble Beach, and it seemed no time at all before they were passing the gate guard with a wave and a smile. Some ten minutes later, Steve swung the car off the road at a point where the Seventeen-Mile Drive gave a panoramic view of the coastline below.

"Thought we'd take a look around from here and decide what sort of setting appeals to us," he said, getting out and coming around to open her door. He held out a hand to help her from the car. "Do you prefer grassy slopes, rocky coves, or sandy beaches?"

Without answering him at once, Kendall adjusted her sunglasses and turned her face into the light wind to gaze silently at the sea. It was a view that she would never get enough of if she lived to be a hundred. A glance at her companion was enough to tell her that he felt much the same way.

The sky was clear except for a few wispy stratus clouds, and sparkling sunlit waves shattered rhythmically against the craggy sentinel rocks in violent, diamond-dusted splashes of white foam before rolling almost lackadaisically up onto the sandy beach. They could see the Pebble Beach Golf Course sprawling below, and Kendall remembered the days when, as teenagers, she and her friends had clambered over the dunes from Carmel Beach to sneak onto the course during the Crosby Tournament. It was only a week or so since this year's tournament had ended, and there were the usual pairs and foursomes there now. It looked like a good day for golf, too, and she glanced again at Steve, remembering that Sylvia Hutton had said he enjoyed the game, and wondering if he wished he were on the course now. But he only grinned down at her before turning away to scan the coastline for a likely picnic spot.

The breeze blowing in from the sea was brisk and chilly, doing its best to nip at her legs through the protective gray wool slacks. The gulls screamed and dove, battling each other for scraps, real or imaginary, and off in the distance, above the thunderous roar of breaking waves, they could hear the barking of sea lions. Taking a deep breath of the salty, damp air, Kendall hugged her maroon blazer more closely around her slim figure and plunged chilled hands into warm pockets.

"Cold?" He moved closer to her, putting an arm around her shoulders and drawing her to him, as though he would share the warmth of his own body with her.

"It is a little chilly," she admitted, snuggling closer. "Rocks, sand, or grassy slopes—we'll have to find a spot that's protected from this wind."

"There's a place just the other side of Pescadero Point that's got a bit of everything," he said. "And from here, it looks like we'll have it to ourselves."

The place he spoke of turned out to be a small sandy cove, dotted with ragged patches of coarse shore grass and well sheltered from the wind by high, craggy rocks. It was pleasant and private. Carefully selecting a site near the rocks but far enough from the waterline so that when the tide turned they would not have to move, they carried blankets from the car and spread out their feast. Steve had even brought plastic champagne glasses for their wine. They made huge sandwiches, piling on the salami and cheese until they could barely get their mouths around the end products, laughing at each other whenever a bit of cheese or meat escaped. But nothing went to waste. Scavenger gulls paced back and forth overhead, swooping down to catch whatever was tossed their way and screeching with outrage when they were ignored.

Once the sandwiches and deliciously gooey eclairs had disappeared, Steve bunched one of the blankets against a convenient rock, lit his pipe, and invited Kendall to lean back with him to enjoy the view. Without a murmur of protest, she snuggled into the crook of his arm and accepted a refill from the wine bottle. She felt wonderfully warm and relaxed, at peace with the whole world. In fact, she thought idly, as aromatic pipe smoke drifted lightly past and Steve's fingers lightly began to caress her shoulder, she would like to make love with him right here on the sand under the golden sun.

But fortunately or unfortunately—she wasn't sure which— the sun was for show purposes only and gave little warmth even to their sheltered nook. He knocked his pipe out at last, scooping sand over the glowing ashes. Then he leaned back again, and his hand moved tantalizingly to the side of her breast. To be sure, she reflected idly, they did have the two blankets. She turned her face up to his. Steve kissed her lightly, then took her glass from her and set it beside his in a cranny in one of the rocks. Turning back without a word, he gathered her closer, dropping another light kiss on her lips.

Then, as he looked searchingly into her eyes, he began to let his hands roam idly, sending delightful shivers through her body.

"Steve," she said breathlessly a few moments later.

"Mmmm?"

"Kiss me properly."

"With pleasure," he replied promptly, his satisfaction at having stirred her self-evident.

He began gently, waiting for her response, but it was not long in coming, and Kendall soon felt as though she were being carried into another life altogether. It was as it always was with him, his kisses and caresses taking her to heights she had never known before. She scarcely noticed his hand at her waist as he began to pull her blouse loose from the waistband of her slacks, but brief moments later, the touch of his fingers against the bare skin of her breast sent shock waves through her as though it were the first time anyone had ever done such a thing. She gasped with the pleasure of it and uttered not a word of protest when he began to unbutton her blouse.

As the afternoon progressed, they alternately sipped their wine, smoked, made idle conversation, and continued their sensual explorations in what often seemed to Kendall to be the tentative, experimental manner she remembered from her high-school days. The illusion was carried even further when they were startled by the sudden sound of voices from just the other side of their sheltering rocks. Both Steve and Kendall sprang apart and began buttoning their clothes with guilty haste.

At the second button, Kendall paused and glanced up at him, merriment twinkling from her eyes. He caught her look and broke into laughter. She joined him, putting her head back and laughing until tears began streaming down her cheeks. Then, suddenly, he reached for her, and she was in his arms again as though there had been no interruption. When she finally came up for air, the voices had faded into the distance.

The fog, which had been threatening for some time, began

to roll in at last, so they packed up their things and drove to Del Monte Lodge to warm themselves in front of the fire with hot rum punches. Then, too soon, it was time for Steve to take Kendall home. She was nearly glad he couldn't stay, because she was sure now that he wouldn't say anything further about taking her to bed, and he certainly hadn't said anything about a permanent relationship of any sort. He didn't even mutter his love for her the way most men did when they were kissing her. And, she thought ruefully, as she watched him drive out of sight, if she weren't careful, she'd be begging him to take her to bed, commitment or no commitment. Then she would despise herself for compromising so easily. Or would she?

She passed the evening restlessly, her thoughts filled with Steve Langston, and Monday morning, Meg was waiting for her when she arrived at the studio. "How was your weekend?" she asked cheerfully.

The question had been anticipated, and Kendall obliged her with a brief description of the drive down the coast. "We were going to have dinner at Nepenthe," she concluded, "but Steve was called back by his office for some sort of emergency, so we had a light supper afterward at my house instead."

"But Jack said—" Meg broke off, flushing. "I mean . . . oh, fiddle! I don't know why I'm carrying on like the other woman or something. There was nothing in it at all."

"Nothing in what?" Kendall asked, smiling. "Sounds like you've already heard about what happened Saturday night."

"Jack called me," Meg admitted. "He must have called right after you tossed him out on his ear, because when I said he could come over he was there almost before I hung up. He needed a shoulder to cry on, and I must say that considering how much you've been seeing of the poor guy, it's no wonder he feels as though you've thrown him over!"

Kendall shook her head. "I've been perfectly frank with Jack all along," she said. "I made it quite clear to him long ago that I wasn't interested in any entanglement. If he's deluded himself into thinking otherwise, it's hardly my fault, is it?"

"I suppose not," Meg said slowly, "but all your men seem to get ideas, no matter what you tell them."

"All my men!" Kendall repeated indignantly. "You say that the same way Steve talks about his 'ladies.' Makes us both sound like we've got harems or something."

Meg chuckled. "Well, you always do have at least one guy on your string, don't you? Steve is probably the same way with women. But Jack's different. That man's really crazy about you."

"No, he's not," Kendall disagreed bluntly. "He only thinks he is. We don't even like the same things. He likes country music and football games and big parties. He even likes boxing matches." She gave a mock shudder. "I like mood music, ballet, Broadway musicals, candlelight suppers, and walks along the beach. I want a man who isn't afraid of me and who can let me enjoy my independence without being intimidated by it. Jack wants someone he can possess, who will depend upon him and cater to his every whim, someone who will love him as much as he loves himself. I'm just not the right person."

"But you've been dating him for months!" Meg protested.

"I know, and I've enjoyed his company," Kendall said. "But I wouldn't want it as a permanent diet. We usually go out to dinner or to a movie. If we talk, it's about cars he's sold or idiotic customers he's dealt with. Some of his stories are really funny, but after a while I'd like to talk politics or economics or just exchange ideas on some current event or other. Jack doesn't think women ought to know about those things, so he laughs off any attempt I make in that direction or else he simply doesn't listen. It's positively infuriating, Meg. I couldn't marry any man who treated me like that."

"Well, I think you're out of your mind. Jack is charming and witty, and he listens to *my* ideas. Not that I like to talk politics or any of that stuff, of course, but he does listen, Kendall. Really, he does. You probably don't give him a chance."

She sounded almost vehement, and Kendall gazed at her thoughtfully, but all she said was, "Perhaps you're right, Meggy. What's on for today?"

Meg accepted the change of subject, and her normally buoyant spirits were quickly restored. They spent the morning at the studio, and there were several calls from potential clients, at least one of whom, a Mrs. Carmody, said she had been referred to them by Stephen Langston. Meg nearly crowed over that one, agreeing that someone would visit the woman that very afternoon to discuss what was needed and to give her a preliminary estimate of the charges.

"That's your job," she told Kendall. Then she frowned. "On the other hand, one of us has to go out to the Sandcastle this afternoon to check on the painters. They're starting to work on the study, you know. But I wanted to visit that fabric place in Pacific Grove to look for material I can use to replace those drapes. I still haven't found exactly what I'm looking for. God knows when those old things were first hung, but it must have been during the forties or early fifties. That sort of muted floral pattern just doesn't exist anymore. If I can't find what I need in that shop, one of us will have to go up to the city. We may even have to custom order the old pattern."

"That won't work," Kendall chuckled. "What you politely call 'muted' is probably only faded, as you must know perfectly well. And why stick to the exact same pattern? I should think anything in those colors or even something a bit brighter would do."

"No, it won't. You may think I'm nuts, Kendall, but that study is one of the most comfortable rooms I've ever been in, and I know Steve likes it the way it is. But the fact is that those drapes are going to crumble to dust any day now, and some poor soul will sit right through that old leather chair or trip on a snag in that threadbare carpet. I want it to look exactly the way it looks now, and that's practically impossible. None of the new stuff will have the lovely mellow quality that can only come with age, so no matter how careful I am, he's going to feel odd in it for a while. I just want to see that he feels as much at home as he can."

"All right, I agree. In that case, you'd better be the one to check on the painters. One of them would start telling me all about how the light will affect one shade or another, and I'd be lost. I'm still no good when it comes to talking technicalities. I'll go see this Mrs. Carmody at one o'clock, and then I'll shoot over to Pacific Grove to check the fabric shop. I know those drapes well enough to bring swatches of anything that looks like being a possibility. Have you got your car today?"

"No, but Aunt Hilda is coming in to town to take me to lunch. She can drive me out to the Sandcastle afterward, and I'll wait for you to pick me up there." Meg grinned. "She wants to find out how her matchmaking is going."

Kendall chuckled, but the thought of Langston brought another upon its heels. "Look here, Meg," she said abruptly, "I don't know how you're going to take this, but Steve is having us followed." Meg's eyes flew open in surprise, and Kendall went on to explain as well as she could. She needn't have worried about how Meg would take it, however.

"Just like James Bond or something!" she exclaimed with a wide grin. "Do you mean there is someone outside right now?"

Kendall nodded, smiling at her friend. "No doubt yours and mine are having coffee and doughnuts together just across the street. You could have asked yours for a ride to the Sandcastle, but unfortunately now you're stuck with Aunt Hilda."

Meg made a rude face but refused to admit that there was anything the least bit bothersome about having a bodyguard. "It makes me feel very important," she said, tilting her nose into the air.

"Well, it makes me wonder just what Steve thinks could happen to us," said Kendall. "And I don't like it. I don't like the feeling of being watched all the time even if the watcher is a friendly sort."

"Oh, pooh, nothing is going to happen," Meg declared

firmly. "That's precisely why they're there, of course. Steve is just being cautious. I suppose in his line of work, caution is second nature. But do you mean to say he's told you nothing about this popular little project of his?"

"Not a word beyond the fact that it's something for the government and something he's particularly interested in."

"How can you stand not to know more than that?" Meg demanded. "I'd be hounding him day and night to tell me all about it."

Kendall shrugged. "I suppose that someday we'll all know about it," she said, "but I can't say that it bothers me particularly not to know right now. And I certainly wouldn't press him to divulge classified information just to satisfy my simple curiosity, or yours."

"No, I suppose not," Meg agreed, though she sounded disappointed.

The matter was dropped, and they spent the rest of the morning busy with various tasks in the studio. Aunt Hilda arrived shortly after noon and exclaimed her pleasure at seeing Kendall again so soon. "You simply must come to lunch with us, my dear," she announced happily.

"I'd love to," Kendall replied, "but it will have to be another time. Your niece has given me errands in another part of the county, and it's high time I was leaving. I think she wanted to be sure I was well out of the way so you could discuss my affairs to your heart's content."

"Such impudence," retorted Miss Quick. "As though we would say anything behind your back that we should hesitate to say to your face. We just want to discuss the best way of approaching matters, that's all."

"Aunt Hilda, do shut up," Meg begged, grinning. "You'll have her taking us much too seriously. She's still not quite used to the way our family operates, you know."

Shaking her head with genuine amusement, Kendall shooed them off to their lunch. It would be totally useless to tell them that her affairs were none of their business. Besides, it was refreshing to know people who were so candid about their interest. If it were known, her relationship with Stephen Langston would provide food for a good many discussions, but how many of her friends would let her know so openly that they meant to talk about her?

CHAPTER 9

Mrs. Carmody proved to be a friendly, cheerful woman who knew exactly what she wanted Blake and Potter to accomplish in her tree-shaded home overlooking the old Del Monte Golf Course. It was a lovely location, Kendall thought, almost as nice as the Pebble Beach area. Standing in Mrs. Carmody's living room and looking out at the thick-growing trees, it was almost possible to imagine what the area must have been like in the heyday of the old Del Monte Hotel, now housing part of the Monterey Naval Postgraduate School, but before World War II one of the most elegant resorts in California.

She spent a pleasant hour with Mrs. Carmody, doing her color analysis and making various annotated sketches and floor plans for Meg's benefit. If Kendall seemed more interested in discussing the man who had recommended Blake and Potter for the job than in obtaining sufficient information to be certain that Mr. Carmody's coloring was similar to his wife's, Mrs. Carmody certainly didn't seem to notice. An estimate was drawn up and accepted, and Kendall went on her way, cheerfully thinking that business was definitely picking up. It was not until she reached her car that it occurred to her to hope that Mr. Carmody would not clash with the colors that would best suit his wife.

The shop in Pacific Grove had a few drapery samples that looked like they might provide possibilities. At least, she thought, eyeing them skeptically, the colors were nearly right. Some were perhaps a bit truer than Meg wanted, but Kendall liked them very much herself and thought they would perk up the study admirably. Whether or not any one pattern would be acceptable to Meg was another matter, of course.

Tossing her package into the car, she drove on to the Sandcastle where she found Meg, Aunt Hilda, and—surprisingly—Sylvia Hutton all sitting around a small table in a dining parlor off the kitchen drinking tea. A plate of brownies and iced petits fours sat in the middle of the table next to the cozy-covered teapot.

"Well, you all look hard at work," she teased. Meg grinned up at her, and so did Miss Quick, but Sylvia's brow was furrowed.

"We have been working very hard, I'll have you know," Meg said with exaggerated dignity. "Sylvia has gone over the finished plans with a fine-tooth comb, and she approved every single detail, so we can go ahead at once. And Aunt Hilda has been over the entire house with me. She says it's very nice."

"Very nice?" She cast a twinkling look at the older woman, who promptly poured her a cup of tea. Kendall dumped her parcel unceremoniously on the table in front of Meg.

"Well, I think she was hoping to discover signs of a ghost or two," Meg explained as she undid the wrapping.

"Aunt Hilda, this is twentieth-century California, not sixteenth-century Britain!"

"Much you know, young lady," said Hilda tartly. "It wouldn't be the first haunted house in the forest, I assure you."

"You're joking!"

"No, she's not," Meg put in. "There was the old Macomber House—you know, the huge one they called the Mystery House. The Macombers built it in 1917 of logs they imported from British Columbia. When it was finished, they spent a whole week there, finishing up with an elaborate dress ball. Then they went away and never came back. There was a caretaker, of course, but the house stood empty for nearly fifty years. It burned down a few years ago."

"Arson," declared Hilda flatly with a grimace of distaste. "Everyone knew it."

"Well, they never caught anyone, so we can't know for sure," Meg said fairly, "but it made one terrific haunted house in its day."

"There's another one, too," Hilda added. "I can't think of the owner's name offhand, but there's a house not far from this one that has a ghost who pops in every once in a while to demand specific renovations. He sticks around until the changes are made, too, so needless to say, his hosts usually obey his wishes."

"Now, he sounds like the sort of ghost whose acquaintance we ought to cultivate," Kendall observed with a chuckle. "We could just commission him to haunt one house after another, provided of course that he strictly agrees to refer all his custom to Blake and Potter."

Meg and Hilda laughed, and Meg observed that she was certain no ghosts would be found haunting the Sandcastle. "Steve would have sent them packing the moment he walked through the door. Don't you agree, Sylvia?"

Miss Hutton nodded absentmindedly, her brow still furrowed. She had been absentmindedly running her finger around the rim of her teacup while they talked. "The only ghost we ever heard of around here is that lady in lace who is supposed to flit about down by the Witch Tree on the Seventeen-Mile Drive. Will you excuse me while I make a phone call?" She got up abruptly and headed toward the kitchen without further comment.

"Kendall, most of these samples won't do," Meg said a moment later. "They are winter shades, not summer. The colors for the drapes need to be more grayed. What on earth were you thinking about when you selected these?"

"They'll fade in time just like the originals did," Kendall replied vaguely, her mind still on Sylvia's odd behavior. "Is it me?" she asked curiously. "I know Steve chewed her out for that business over the study, but I didn't expect her to react like this."

"It's not that," Meg said, giving her a long, measuring look. "She's worried."

"About what?" Then a sudden, dismaying thought occurred to her. "His plane isn't overdue, is it? I didn't think he meant to return for a couple of days at least."

"The plane's fine," Meg said quickly. "But Steve's not. He got back about two o'clock, and Sylvia says he's sick. But evidently he's the type who won't admit it. Hates doctors and fuss."

Kendall nodded, remembering the scene over the dentist when she had first met him. "But he was fine yesterday," she protested feebly.

"Maybe so. But he's not fine now. I can't imagine Sylvia getting into such a snit over a matter of a few sniffles either. She's really worried. I don't think she would have sat down at all if Aunt Hilda hadn't been here. She really wanted to get straight back to the office as soon as she'd finished checking over the work sheets."

Sylvia came back in just then, but it did not seem as though her worry had been eased by the call. Meg asked if everything was all right, and she shrugged, taking her place at the table again and saying quietly, "You'll be able to see for yourself in a few moments. He's on his way here."

Kendall was conscious of a sudden sense of delight that couldn't be repressed, but then she realized that Sylvia was even more worried than she had been before. "You act as if it's odd that he should be coming home," she observed, forcing a note of calm into her voice.

"It *is* odd. Sandra said he means to fly to L.A. tonight, and that he is coming home to pack. He knows I'm here, and I nearly always see to his packing for these trips. And even if he didn't want me to do it this time," she added with a trace of bitterness, "Nelly and Charlotte have both done it before, and I could certainly have taken his suitcase back to the office. He has a pile of work to finish before he goes, and I know he had no intention earlier of coming here. It's almost as though he's lost track of what he's doing."

A cold chill raced down Kendall's spine at these words, but she forced herself to consider that Sylvia was probably going through some sort of emotional crisis herself that might lead her to interpret Langston's actions more dramatically than she would otherwise have done. The thought sustained her only until his arrival.

Jerry was with him, and they came in quickly, startling the three at the table.

"Sylvia! What the devil are you doing here? I thought I left you in charge at the office."

"I've been here nearly two hours, Steve," Sylvia said carefully. "I told you where I would be before I left. Would you like something to eat?"

"No time for that," he said, chopping his words as though the time taken to enunciate them was too precious to be wasted. "Got to pack."

"Nelly is attending to it," Sylvia replied, keeping her voice even, almost soothing.

Kendall was watching Steve. His color was abnormally high, his skin seemed to be stretched across his cheekbones, and his eyes had a shiny, nearly glazed look about them. His movements were almost frenetic. She glanced at Jerry. His lips were pursed, his forehead creased. There could be no doubt that he was worried.

"You've got time for a drink, boss," he said now. "Got to wait for the bags anyway. You might as well sit down and relax for a few minutes."

"I want to see what in blazes they're up to in the study," Steve said suddenly, turning on his heel and striding rapidly from the room. Jerry cast a helpless glance at Sylvia, then moved to follow him.

"Just a minute, Jerry," Kendall found herself saying. "Why don't you let me take a stab at it. Maybe I can at least get him to sit down. He looks like he needs a sedative, so you go ahead and fix him a strong gin and tonic. I just might be able to get it down him." She looked at Sylvia to see if there would be any argument from that quarter, but Sylvia only nodded, causing

Kendall to feel real fear for the first time. If Sylvia was worried enough to turn matters over to someone else, then she must be very worried indeed! She practically jumped up from the table and hurried off in Steve's wake, but she didn't catch up with him until he had reached the study.

He stood in the doorway, watching the painters with a jaundiced eye. "They're really making a muck of things in there, aren't they?" he growled.

"It will be fine when it's done," she soothed. "So, now that you've looked, come back to the living room and have a drink with me. I've been out charging around Monterey and Pacific Grove all afternoon, and I'm thirsty."

She put her hand on his arm, and he looked down at it curiously as though he didn't quite know what to make of the gesture. Then he looked at her, and his eyes finally seemed to focus.

"Kendall. What are you doing here?"

"Silly, I work here from time to time, remember?"

He nodded, and she slipped her arm through his, drawing him steadily toward the living room. He moved obediently enough, though he didn't speak again, and he matched his pace to hers without difficulty. The frenetic activity that had worried her so much seemed to have burned itself out for the moment.

Jerry was waiting for them, and Sylvia and Meg were talking in the corner. Gratefully, Kendall noted that Jerry had had sense enough to concoct a drink for her as well as for his boss. She had feared a reaction should Steve see only the one drink waiting. Relaxing now, she walked with him toward the sofa, but just as she thought she had him well in hand, he stopped still in his tracks.

"I've got to go," he said politely to the room at large. "Got a pile of business to attend to, then a long flight to L.A. Sorry to have to cut this little party short. Be seeing you." He turned abruptly to leave.

"Steve!" Kendall snapped his name at him, and it had the desired effect insofar as it made him turn back, but he seemed to be in a complete daze. She moved to take his arm again, but this time he pulled away from her, looking down at her as though she were a stranger. Then Jerry started to move toward them, and Langston glanced quickly at him and frowned. A hint of fear glinted in his eyes just before they glazed over again and he crumpled to the floor at Kendall's feet.

Someone cried out, and Kendall dropped to her knees beside him, her stomach tightening with fear. He was only unconscious for seconds before his eyes flickered open again, and he looked up at her through what seemed to be mists of confusion. "I love you," he said clearly, almost forcefully. Kendall stared at him, nearly as bewildered as he had seemed to be just a moment before.

"He's raving," Sylvia said bluntly from directly behind her.

Steve's vague gaze drifted to Sylvia. "Can't do the job properly," he muttered with near anger. "Got to get . . ." The words fluttered in the air for a moment before he passed out again, and Kendall looked back at Sylvia, whose face had gone perfectly white.

"You're right, Sylvia," she said crisply. "He's completely delirious. Call a doctor at once." She put her hand on Steve's forehead. "Wait! He's burning up with fever. Perhaps you'd better make that an ambulance. Move!" Sylvia seemed to shake herself and hurried to the phone. But a moment later, Kendall heard her request Security and realized she was not calling the ambulance, after all. She turned to Jerry. "Get me some ice. We've got to do what we can to bring his fever down. I'm sure it's dangerous. And tell Nelly to bring some blankets, too. I don't want him going into shock on us. Meg, where's Aunt Hilda?"

"She went home," Meg said quietly. "Said we would handle things much better here without her."

"Just as well," Kendall agreed. "Get over there and tell Sylvia to get help. Steve needs a doctor a whole lot more than he needs a stupid security cop!"

"Sylvia is just following Steve's orders, Miss Blake," Jerry said quietly from the bar, where he was filling plastic bags with tiny ice cubes. "Nelly will bring the blankets. Where do you want this ice?"

Sylvia turned from the phone just then. "Jerry, Dr. Weatherby is at the Cypress Point course. His office says he should be just about at the third tee by now, and they will bleep him. If you hurry, you'll get to the clubhouse about the same time he does. Bring him."

"Right you are," Jerry agreed, handing Kendall the ice bags and hurrying to the door.

Before the doctor arrived, Steve slipped in and out of consciousness several times, mumbling odds and ends of sentences each time he struggled to the surface, but none of it made any sense to Kendall. They managed to get him up onto the longer sofa when Dr. Weatherby arrived, and after a brief examination, the doctor said there was no reason why he should not simply be put to bed in his own house.

"Provided you can keep him there," he added sternly. "There's nothing wrong with him but a nasty virus infection that I can see. The fever seems to have reached its peak already and ought to burn itself out before morning. I can dose him to bring it down in the meantime and give him some medication for his aches and pains—believe me, he's got them—but these virus things just have to run their course. Nothing else to do. Couldn't do more in a hospital. Watch his breathing, of course. If it looks like he's having difficulties we'll have to retrench a bit. But he's made of whipcord, that one. He'll be up and about in a day or so— against doctor's orders, mind you, but he'll be up."

"But what if he won't stay in bed?" Sylvia asked, her tone speaking clearly of past experience.

The doctor grinned at her. "Just you tell your boss, young lady, that if he gets any such stupid notions, you'll warn those Army security types that he's still likely to go bonkers on them. They'll slap him into a hospital where they can watch him quicker than a cat can wink her eye. I know how those fellows operate, and so does he. He'll behave."

Sylvia nodded, and a few moments later, Kendall was able to see the truth of the doctor's words when two men in khaki uniforms were ushered into the living room. They spoke quietly with Sylvia, and after a moment or so the younger of the two, an Army captain sporting shiny double bars on his shoulders, glanced at the semi-conscious Langston appraisingly before turning back to continue his discussion with Sylvia. Finally, however, they helped Jerry move him up to the master bedroom, and Sylvia turned to Meg and Kendall.

"They have asked that you stay here until they can talk with you. I told them that he didn't say anything they need to be concerned about, but the rules of the game require that they speak to anyone who was present. I hope you don't mind."

"Of course not," Meg assured her. Kendall said nothing. She wondered what was going on upstairs right now. She felt helpless and numb. Meg was still speaking. "Will those men stay with him?"

"Yes," Sylvia replied. "I wish I could stay, too, but I've got to get back to the office and start calling people. That meeting in L.A. is really important. We've had some odd things going on lately that may require some changes in our security procedures. Since Steve can't go, I'll have to, and Jerry will have to go with me. But I don't like leaving Steve alone. Even with those men up there—or maybe especially because they are there—he's likely to throw a fit when that fever wears off, and I'd hate to think how those two would handle him. No matter what the doctor says, I think Steve could con them into thinking he's okay. Then he'll be up and about until he collapses again."

"I'll stay." To her own astonishment, Kendall heard the words coming from her own mouth. The other two looked at her with widened eyes, as surprised as she was herself, but then Sylvia nodded.

"I'd appreciate it, Miss Blake."

"Kendall."

"Right." Sylvia gave her a steady look. Then she said quietly, "Look, I've got to get going. Would you walk out to my car with me?" Kendall nodded, and Sylvia turned to Jerry. "I'll meet you back at the office, mister. And hustle. The plane's ready when we are."

Kendall followed her slender, well-tailored figure down the corridor and out the front door to a sleek little flame red Porsche parked in the gravel drive. Sylvia tossed her purse and slim leather briefcase in through the car's open window. Then she turned to face Kendall.

"I owe you an apology," she said frankly. "That stunt I pulled the other day was childish and uncalled-for, and I guess you know I got my ears pinned back for it. Nothing less than I deserved, mind you, but I want you to know there are no hard feelings. I didn't realize until he started roaring at me how much Steve cares about you. Just thought you were another one of his ladies who wanted to play house or something. The funny thing is that I'm not sure he knows how much he cares, even yet."

"What do you mean?" Kendall asked, striving to keep her leaping emotions under control.

"It's difficult to explain what I mean if you don't already know," was the blunt reply. "Steve is an incredibly talented and ambitious man. He doesn't have time for much of anything else. But I think you're special to him. That's all. Don't, for pity's sake, take what he said back there too seriously. He really was delirious, and you'd be amazingly foolish to put much faith in his words—just as foolish as I'd be to believe he meant what he said to me. Mind you," she added with a wry smile, "I mean to cause major ructions in Los Angeles, if necessary, to show him that I *can* do the job."

Kendall shot the other girl a rueful look. "I think I owe you an apology, too. At first I thought you wanted to marry Steve, whether to further your own ambition or for other reasons; then I decided you were too ambitious even to think about anyone but yourself. But I'm rapidly coming to believe that you really care about him. You do, don't you."

"Of course I do. I love him," Sylvia responded with a laugh.

"He's my ideal man, and if I were the least bit interested in going the housewife route, I might even make a push to turn his interest toward marriage. But I'm not, and Steve would never countenance a wife whose career is as demanding as mine is. And when push comes to shove, I'll take my career any day. If you ever doubt that, remember that I didn't think twice today about whether I should be at his bedside or in Los Angeles." She winked and slid into the car. "Take care of him, Kendall. Lots of very talented people depend upon him!"

And with that, she started the engine, slipped the car into gear, and rolled off toward the opening gates, leaving Kendall to stare thoughtfully after her.

Walking back into the house, Kendall found her thoughts tumbling over themselves as she tried to make sense of the things Sylvia Hutton had said to her. Did the other girl mean Steve was in love with her or not? And whatever she meant, what was the truth of the matter? Could it be possible that he did love her? And even if that were possible, what exactly did it mean? One thing Sylvia had said stood out above everything else, because Kendall knew it was true. Steve Langston was an extraordinarily talented and ambitious man who had little time in his life for anything beyond his far-reaching business interests. He simply didn't seem to have time to devote to a wife and children.

She met Jerry on his way out and exchanged a polite phrase or two, then returned to her thoughts without any real notion of what she might have said to him. She knew what she wanted. For the past few days she had been, one way or another, denying the truth of it, but that had all gone by the wayside the moment Langston had collapsed at her feet. At that moment, she had known beyond any shadow of doubt that she loved him, that she wouldn't want to plod out the rest of her life without him beside her. The suggestion that he was special had been in her mind since the instant she first laid eyes upon him. That couldn't be denied. But accepting the notion that she actually loved the man was something altogether different. And now that she had accepted it, what next?

Meg was talking with the young Army captain in the living room. The other man, a sergeant, was nowhere to be seen, so she presumed he must be upstairs looking after Steve. She hesitated in the doorway, not knowing whether she should intrude or not, and Meg saw her.

"Come on in, Kendall. This is Captain Curtis."

The young man smiled shyly. "Yes, please do come in, Miss Blake. This is all very routine, you know. Just precautionary stuff. I've already come to the conclusion that Mr. Langston didn't say anything worrisome."

Kendall sat on the smaller sofa. "He didn't say anything at all that I could make head or tail of," she said. "But then I sincerely doubt that I'd understand anything he might say about the project, you know."

"Very likely not." Despite his shyness, he seemed the solid, capable sort, and she liked him. "I understand that you mean to stay here tonight, Miss Blake. That's perfectly all right, of course. We will stay until he has completely recovered his senses, but we'll try not to get in the way."

"You won't be in the way," she observed with a touch of wry amusement. "If what Miss Hutton tells me is correct, we'll all have our hands full keeping him in bed. You will probably be very helpful."

He smiled again. "Glad to do whatever we can. It's a privilege to meet Mr. Langston. Until this last project he hasn't been much of a security risk. Most of the time the head of a large company like Langston Industries has really very little to do with the nitty-gritty, you know, so it isn't necessary for him to have anything but a sort of honorary clearance or two. Mr. Langston, in this instance, is a bit different. As I understand it, this project began as his baby, and he has insisted upon staying right on top of matters all along. To tell the truth," he added confidingly, "I don't even know what the project is exactly. No need for me to know. I just know that it's very hush-hush stuff, so my job is to make sure he doesn't inadvertently disclose something while he doesn't know what he's doing."

After Meg left, Kendall went upstairs with Captain Curtis to find Steve sleeping soundly, the sergeant reading a magazine in a nearby chair. Curtis said they meant to spell each other until the fever broke, so Kendall left them to it for the time being and went to see how much progress the painters had made in the study.

They had departed for the day, the first coat finished, and except for the paint-daubed canvas covering the furniture in the center, the room looked crisp and clean. They would no doubt finish the next day, and she knew Meg had ordered the carpet to be laid on Friday. Then the painters would return the following week to begin work on the rest of the house. Also, she thought cynically, to touch up the baseboards in the study after the carpet layers had done their worst.

She had a light supper in the little dining parlor off the kitchen, and after she had eaten, she went back upstairs to see how her patient was doing. The effects of the sedative were beginning to wear off, and he tossed and turned restlessly. She could tell, too, that the fever was up again, but it would be at least half an hour before they could give him more medication, so she held a metaphorical breath, hoping he wouldn't become too difficult in the meantime.

It took their combined efforts to get the medication down him when the time finally came for it, and the same held true four hours later, but when Kendall struggled awake at four-thirty to see that he got the next dose, he was sleeping peacefully. The sergeant obligingly held him up so that she could give him the medicine, but Steve accepted it easily enough and seemed to know what he was doing when she offered him a glass of water afterward. He wasn't by any means awake, however, and he settled back immediately into deep slumber, but she was fairly certain that the high fever had broken at last. The sergeant agreed.

"We could probably be on our way, miss," he said in an undertone as they moved away from the bed. "But the captain's been up several nights running now, and he could do with a bit of shut-eye. He just dropped off a few moments before you came in, so I guess we'll hang around till Mr. Langston wakes up. But it's safe enough for me to leave him now, even if you want to stay, so if you don't mind, I think I'll grab a catnap, too."

Kendall nodded. It didn't seem the least bit odd to her that she should be alone in Langston's bedroom with him. For that matter, it hadn't seemed odd to be taking care of him with the help of two near strangers. The whole business had seemed perfectly natural. She sat down wearily in the chair vacated by the sergeant, leaned back, and surveyed the sleeping figure in the bed.

He looked so peaceful, almost vulnerable. A lock of dark hair had fallen over one eye, and she nearly leaned forward to brush it away. But it would probably only fall back again. Much better to take what opportunity she had to think about what lay ahead.

She loved him. The thought settled in, warm and cozy, not the least bit diminished by her near certainty that the relationship would fail to develop the way she would like it to. But since she had come to the conclusion that he would never want a permanant relationship, perhaps it was time to deal with her own feelings about that. Would she, out of her love for him, be willing to settle for anything less? Her principles, after all, were not set in granite. They weren't even something she had consciously mapped out for herself. She had simply assumed that one day she would marry and have children, and she tended to judge the men she dated on that basis. It had always worked before. But this time, she had to deal with the fact that Steve had almost certainly not even considered the possibility of marrying her. She was not even sure he would be willing to make any sort of commitment to a relationship. So now what? she wondered. She could hardly deny that the magic spark was there. Just his presence in the same room nearly sent her emotions into orbit.

She sighed, settling herself more comfortably and staring

at a point high on the wall above the bed. Supposing she did give in to him. Just how would she go about it? Wait for him to make another pass and just melt submissively in his arms? By the look of things, that pass might be a long time coming. And she simply couldn't tell him that she now knew him well enough to let him do whatever he liked. It would sound as though he had had to pass some sort of test. Besides, her better self clamored rebelliously at the mere thought of such a scene. The awful thing was that, no matter what she did now, there really was no way she could give in without . . . well . . . giving in. And *that* would merely reinforce his arrogant attitude and place her right in the midst of the rest of his "ladies." She didn't think she could bear that.

Alternately dozing and struggling with wayward thoughts, she passed the next few hours in restless discomfort until sunlight began to creep in through the eastern windows. A shaft of light struck her eye just as she was waking again, and she started slightly. Then her thoughts came rushing back, and she glanced at the figure in the bed to discover, disconcertingly, that he was looking back at her. He was lying on his back, and he seemed to have propped another pillow behind himself.

CHAPTER 10

Steve's gaze was clear and direct. "Good morning," he said.
"Would you like to explain how I come to be here instead of
. . . where am I supposed to be, anyway?"

"Los Angeles," she replied, sitting up straighter in her
chair. "But it's all right. Sylvia and Jerry went."

"I wondered. I just have a vague memory of somebody
saying something about a meeting, but that's it. I don't really
remember coming home. Did I? On my own, I mean. Or did
somebody bring me from the office? And—most important of
all—why are you here? Not that I'm not delighted to see you,
of course. But I confess to a certain amount of curiosity."

"You got here pretty much on your own," she answered
carefully, "and I'm here because everyone was afraid you
would try to get up too soon."

"Did you think you could stop me?" There was a lazy,
teasing note in his voice.

"I don't know," she answered honestly. "I hope you won't
be stupid enough to get up before the doctor says you may,
because if you do, you'll very likely end up back in bed in
worse shape than you were in before. You might even find
yourself in a hospital. But if you insist upon being an idiot, I
don't suppose there would be much I could do about it by
myself."

Langston grimaced. "You don't pull your punches, do you?
Supposing I were to offer a deal?"

She eyed him warily. "What sort of a deal?"

But he didn't answer directly. "Have you been here all
night?" She nodded. "Did you sleep?"

She shook her head. "Not much."

"You look it. Go to bed. Any of the guest rooms will do. They are always kept ready for unexpected company." She opened her mouth to protest, and grinning, he held up a restraining hand. "That's my best offer. You go get some beauty sleep, and I'll stay put till that quack Weatherby shows up. I assume he means to show up sometime this morning?" She nodded again. The doctor had said quite clearly that he meant to stop by before noon to see how his patient was progressing. "Okay. That's the deal. You sleep, I stay put. You don't sleep, I get up. And I don't mind admitting I'd just as soon stay put for a while. I feel like Muhammad Ali must have felt after his fight with Larry Holmes."

"I don't know much about boxing," Kendall confessed, wishing for the first time that she did know more, "but he lost that one, didn't he?"

"He did. It was his last fight."

There was a light tap on the door, and young Captain Curtis put his head in. "Heard voices, and just wanted to let you know we're leaving, Miss Blake. Good morning, sir. You're looking a good deal more chipper today."

"Good grief!" Langston snorted. "Did Sylvia bring in the troops?"

"Just precautionary, sir," Curtis smiled. "You'll be glad to know we might just as well have stayed home."

Langston did look as though he was rather pleased with himself, Kendall thought, watching him fondly. Then, as Curtis took his leave and the intensely blue eyes turned back toward her, she schooled her features to their usual placid expression.

"Well?" he said pointedly. "What about it?"

She stood up. "I'll do as you suggest," she agreed with ironic emphasis on the final word, "although I'm sure your methods are nothing less than extortionate. However, I didn't stay here all night merely to indulge myself in the questionable pleasure of arguing you into another fever. Are you hungry?"

"Famished. Nelly ought to be wandering around up here

somewhere by now. Tell her to get Mrs. Foster to rustle me up some bacon and eggs."

She nodded and went to find Nelly, adding orange juice to his menu and telling the maid, quite unfairly she realized, to see that he drank it. "He needs vitamins, Nelly," she added lamely in response to the look of dismay with which her order was received. Then she smiled. "Just do your best."

Nelly permitted herself a small, long-suffering sigh, but she responded, as nearly everyone did, to Kendall's smile. A few moments later, Kendall found herself in a guest room down the hall from the master suite. The room boasted its own attached bathroom, so she stripped off her clothes, stepped gratefully into the white-tiled shower, and turned the water on full-blast to let the pounding hot spray do its best to relax some of her aching muscles. Once she was dry again, she set the alarm of the little flowered clock on the bedside table for noon, slipped into the bed, and dropped off to sleep almost immediately.

She awoke to the tinkling notes of a cheery Swiss folk tune. Stretching languidly, she turned to stare at the little clock. The tune came to an end and began again. Smiling, she reached out to touch the alarm button. The music stopped. It was certainly a far nicer way to wake up than that provided by her Big Ben, which startled her rudely out of slumber if her inner alarm failed to wake her that split second before it went off.

She got up, dressed quickly, and finding a hairbrush on the dressing table, brushed her raven curls until they shone. Then she added lipstick and, peering critically at her reflection, decided her appearance would have to do. She certainly looked a good deal better than when she had come to bed.

Walking quickly down the hall to the master suite, she was astonished to find the door open and the bed freshly made. But then, hadn't everyone warned her that he would never stay put? Therefore, the anger rising in her breast was completely unreasonable. She knew it, and she fought against the feeling; yet her eyes were glittering when she hurried downstairs, scarcely knowing whether she expected to find him there or not.

He was in the living room, standing near the huge window overlooking the sea, and he was dressed in an expertly cut and tailored blue gray, three-piece suit. Kendall's breath caught in her throat at the sight of him.

"Well, good afternoon, Sleeping Beauty," he greeted her, smiling. "I must say you look a darn sight better with a little color in your cheeks."

"Never mind how I look!" she snapped. "You're supposed to be in bed."

"I've already been there," he said, eyes twinkling. "I found that it grew a mite tiresome after a while."

"But our deal!"

"Weatherby's in there," he replied, nodding toward the kitchen. "Nelly thinks Mrs. Foster might well be coming down with my bug."

At that moment, the doctor entered the room. "She's all right, Steve," he said with a chuckle. "Just been dieting more than is good for her. I told her off, and Nelly's got her sitting down with a nice poached egg and a piece of toast. Best medicine she could have. Good day to you, young lady," he added when he became aware of Kendall's presence.

"Doctor Weatherby, did you tell him he ought to get up?" she demanded.

"Nope. Told him he should stay in bed at least until tomorrow morning," replied the doctor. "He's got the constitution of a rogue elephant, but he's not out of the woods yet, and he should take it easy. Might as well talk to my plants as to him, though. At least I get a more positive response from them."

"You got a positive response from me, too, you old quack," Steve teased. "I said I was *positively* going to go check things out at the office."

The levity was too much for Kendall. "How dare you talk to him that way!" she flashed. "He only wants you to be sensible for once in your life. You're spoiled rotten, Steve

Langston—always insisting upon getting your own way, no matter who gets hurt. You scared everyone silly yesterday, and now you seem to think it's your prerogative to do it again. This is just plain stubborn childishness. You may pretend to be a grown man, but right now you're acting exactly like a ten-year-old brat who needs a good—" She broke off, amazed at herself. A glance at the doctor told her that he was surprised, too, but also a little amused. Langston was not amused.

"I'll say what I jolly well feel like saying!" he rapped out, temper flaring. "To him or to anyone else. And 'sensible' is what *I* decide it is. I'm perfectly all right, and I've got no time to waste being mollycoddled and fussed over. Not you, not the doctor, not anyone is going to tell me how to behave or what I might or might not need. Do you understand all that I'm saying to you, Miss Blake?"

"Perfectly, Mr. Langston," she responded icily, reaching for her purse. "It really is most unfortunate that no one ever took the trouble to teach you how to show consideration for others. I only hope that the next time you fall flat on your arrogant face there is still someone around who cares enough to help you get to your feet again."

Without looking to see his reaction to her angry words, she slung her purse over her shoulder and strode quickly from the room. As she reached the front door, she thought she heard him call to her, but she did not pause to find out. Her eyes burning with unshed tears, she found her car keys and was soon driving through the gates. Then the tears began to flow in steady streams, making it difficult for her to see where she was going. Furiously, she brushed her sleeve across her eyes, but the gesture cleared her vision for only a moment.

Ahead on the left she recognized the little lane that led to Hilda Quick's house, and without really thinking why, she turned the Camaro up the hill and, moments later, into Hilda's driveway. Then she just sat, rubbing at her eyes, forcing her emotions under control again. When she was

quite sure she could manage, she opened the car door and
climbed out to stand in the sunlit driveway.

Drawing a deep breath of the crisp, fresh air, she turned
resolutely toward the house. She was starving. That's all
that's wrong, she told herself firmly. Not enough sleep. No
food. It was simple. A cup of tea and one of Hilda's muffins
would put her right again. Hilda made wonderfully delicious
muffins.

Slowly, she made her way up the steps to the deck, then to
the front door. What if Hilda wasn't home? Somehow the
thought was unbearably depressing. What on earth was
wrong with her?

She knocked lightly, then—with impatience—rang the
bell. Quick, sharp steps sounded on the other side of the door,
and Kendall found herself sighing with relief. The door
opened, and Hilda greeted her with a smile that changed
rapidly to an expression of deep concern.

"Kendall, child, what on earth is the matter!" She took
Kendall's arm and drew her into the entryway. "You look
dreadful. What's happened? Is Mr. Langston worse than they
thought he was? Good grief! He hasn't died, has he?"

"No, no, he's all right. At least, he *says* he's all right. But,
oh, Aunt Hilda," she went on in a rush, "the doctor says he
isn't, and he was so sick, and now he says he's going to the
office, and the doctor says he shouldn't, that he should be in
bed, and—"

"Whoa there!" Hilda interjected. "Slow down. Better yet,
come in and sit down. You seem to be at the end of your
tether, child. When did you last eat?"

When did she eat? Kendall had to concentrate in order to
answer the simple question. "I . . . dinner, I guess. I
thought I was hungry when I got here, but I don't think I can
eat. My insides seem to be jumping all over the place."

"Nerves!" scoffed Hilda. "And you, of all people. Always
thought you were too self-possessed to indulge yourself in
this sort of hysterical behavior."

The words and the challenging look that accompanied

them had their effect. Letting out a long sigh, Kendall took herself in hand, meeting that look with a rueful one of her own. "I am being silly, aren't I? I can't think what's gotten into me lately. I never seem to know what's going to happen next."

"Well, the first thing that's going to happen is that you are going to sit down to a proper meal," Hilda said practically. "I was just going to fix myself a bite anyway, so you come on in and sit at the table while I whip up a little something. You can tell me whatever you want to tell me from there."

Kendall took off her jacket and dropped it over the back of a chair on her way through the sitting room to the dining alcove. There was hot coffee already made, so Hilda plunked a steaming mug down in front of her and handed her the cream and sugar, ordering her firmly to "jazz it up a lot."

Obediently, Kendall stirred in a teaspoon of sugar and a splash of cream, then went on stirring absentmindedly while she tried to put her thoughts in order. Purr-See padded over hospitably to lean against her legs, stroking himself back and forth against them until it became obvious that she wasn't in a mood to converse with him. Twitching one pink-tipped ear in disgust, he stepped away and, with fluid grace, ascended to the seat of the chair next to hers, where he turned in three precise circles before settling comfortably, his paws tucked under his thickly furred chest, to stare at her unblinkingly.

Within minutes, the appetizing smell of ham and onions began to drift into the room from the kitchen. "Tell me about Mr. Langston," Hilda prompted, her words accompanied by various intriguing sizzles and pops. "What exactly did the doctor say, anyway? I spoke to Meg last night, of course, but she only said they thought it was one of those nasty viral infections, and that Mr. Langston ought to shake it off without much trouble. I gather," she added dryly, "that he has done just that."

"He's being altogether stubborn and stupid about it," said Kendall flatly, as she watched the smoothly efficient motions with which Hilda cracked and beat several eggs, minced bell pepper, and dropped thick slices of bread into the toaster. It was relaxing to watch her, and she no longer wondered whether or not she had an appetite. "The doctor warned him that he ought to stay in bed, but he just thumbed his nose at him and said he'd do as he pleased, thank you. I've never been so furious with anyone in my life!"

"But why should that make you angry?" Hilda asked with simple curiosity. "Mr. Langston is a grown man, after all. Surely, he ought to be allowed to take the responsibility for his own actions."

"He is acting like a ch—" Hilda appeared in the doorway just then with their plates, and Kendall caught sight of the twinkle lurking in her blue eyes and broke off, feeling sudden, revealing warmth creeping up her cheeks. The fluffy, plate-filling Denver omelet that was placed in front of her diverted her attention, however, and it took an effort to wait politely until Hilda had taken the opposite chair and plopped a basket of spicy-smelling muffins down between them before she began to eat.

Hilda lifted her own fork, then paused, clearing her throat ostentatiously. Purr-See turned his head to blink at her, regarded her steady, disapproving gaze with innocent curiosity for a brief moment or two, then with unimpaired dignity, slid from his chair and strode majestically to the hearth, where he proceeded to clean himself in aloof solemnity.

Watching him with appreciation, Kendall chuckled, then turned her attention to her plate. "This is delicious, Aunt Hilda," she said after a short, companionable silence. "Just what the doctor ordered." But then she was self-consciously silent again for a moment or two. "All right," she said then, although Hilda had not spoken, "I'm overreacting. I know I am, but I can't seem to help it. I care about him. I've got no business trying to interfere, and I can't think why I bother, but I do. For that matter, I can't think why I came here to bore you with my emotional upsets," she added helplessly.

"You came," said Hilda with measured firmness, "because you needed to come. That's what families are for, you know, to be there when you need them. And say what you like about it, you are family."

"Thank you, but I still feel as though I've behaved rather badly."

Hilda gave a knowing little shake of her neatly coiffed head, but characteristically she offered no advice, nor did she press Kendall to say more than she wanted to say. They finished their meal with little more than comfortable small talk. Then Kendall had a cigarette with her second cup of coffee, and by the time she said good-bye, she was feeling much more her normal self.

"See," she murmured aloud as she got back into the car and slipped on her sunglasses. "Tea—well coffee, then—and a muffin. That's all it took." Plus a sympathetic ear and an astringent word or two, added the little voice in the back of her head. She smiled at herself, turning the Camaro back into the lane and heading toward Carmel again.

It was nearly four o'clock, and she thought seriously about driving straight home, but then she decided that she really ought to check in at the studio. She knew Meg had had a number of appointments and errands mapped out for the day, but was certain she would be back now and would be wanting to know how things had progressed at the Sandcastle in her absence.

Sally Hunt was just clearing her desk, preparing to leave for the day, but she greeted Kendall with a grin and told her Meg was in the workroom. "There are a couple of messages on your desk," she added. "I'll see you tomorrow."

Kendall lifted a hand in farewell, called out to Meg that she was in, and then stepped to her desk to check the messages. One was from a client, and the other—she allowed herself a small grimace—the other was from Steve. She dropped both messages back on her desk, left a memo for Sally regarding the client, then wandered back to the workroom. Meg was at the drafting table, a full-room sketch in front of her, and she was carefully attaching samples of wallpaper, carpeting, and upholstery fabrics to it. She looked up with a grin.

"Did you call Steve?"

"No. I'll do it later."

"Well, I wish you'd do it now," Meg retorted. "Sally said he's been trying to reach you all afternoon, and I spoke to him myself the last time he called. He didn't say much of any consequence, but he sure sounded angry. Has something happened between you two?"

"I'll call him later," Kendall insisted repressively. "What's that you're doing?"

Meg gave a sigh of resignation, then her grin popped out again. "I think I've got this thing licked," she said, and Kendall realized that the sketch was one of the Sandcastle's living rooms. She wandered over to have a closer look.

"Just look at that paper," Meg said, glowing. "Isn't it wild? Here, don't look at that smidgeon on the sketch. I've got a two-foot hunk right here off the roll." She held it up in front of her.

Kendall looked. She knew Meg had been vaguely thinking of muted stripes in tones to suggest the colors inside an abalone shell, but this wasn't anything so unobtrusive as muted stripes. Far from it. It was, instead, a sort of shiny metallic stuff with big splashes that looked like open sea anemones. The colors were exactly what Meg had said she wanted, and the splashes blended into each other, so the pattern didn't look like merely a bunch of big circles, but Kendall stared at it skeptically.

"Are you sure about this, Meg?"

Meg chuckled. "I knew you'd lose the faith, oh Doubting Thomasina, but mark my words, it will be blooming perfect. Trust me. Once this elegant stuff is on the walls, all those splashes will melt right into the background. You'll be conscious only of the full effect. It won't do to let Steve see it before it's up, however. He'd throw a fit. The problem is that I haven't quite thought how to get around that. The paperhangers would come tomorrow if we could just get the go-ahead." She paused, frowning thoughtfully. "It's a shame Sylvia won't be back before Wednesday. I could handle her."

"Go ahead with it," Kendall said crisply. "If anyone gets huffy, tell them I ordered it. He can bellow at me all he wants to." She turned away, suddenly conscious of incipient tears again, and Meg came instantly to her feet.

"Kendall, what's the matter? And where have you been all day? Since Steve's been calling here all afternoon, I know you haven't been at the Sandcastle."

"I went to Hilda's for lunch," Kendall replied, stifling the tears and turning back to face Meg. She would have liked the subject to end there, but Meg wouldn't allow it, so she soon found herself trying to explain what had happened. It seemed very difficult, as though nothing she said really made any sense. Totally certain that she must sound demented, she nevertheless made the attempt, and Meg listened carefully. When Kendall had finished, Meg said very little beyond agreeing that Steve's behavior must have been particularly maddening.

"Tell you what," she said then. "We haven't gone out on the town for ages. What do you say to a little supper at the Pine Inn? We'll just relax, have a drink, and indulge ourselves in a steak or something."

Kendall smiled gratefully. Meg had said no more about phoning Steve, and she really couldn't talk to him right now. If he was still angry—and by the sound of it, he was—she would no doubt end any conversation they had in tears, and she didn't want to do that. She accepted Meg's invitation with forced cheer and by the time she finished her second drink had mentally scolded herself into a much better frame of mind. With an excellent dinner under her belt, she said good night to Meg at last and drove home, confident that she could handle Mr. Stephen Langston no matter what sort of temper tantrum he chose to throw.

She pulled into the carport, smiling at the friendly light glowing through the living-room drapes. Then, locking the car, she found the gate key and held it poised as she walked up the hill. Approaching the gate, she had an odd sensation that something was amiss, but it was not until after she had opened the gate itself that she realized what was wrong. The light was out in the walkway. So much for photoelectric cells, she thought. Odd though, that a light bulb installed just days ago had burned out already.

"Don't make a sound, Miss Blake, if you want to go on breathing."

The rasping voice came out of the thick blackness ahead of her, and Kendall nearly jumped out of her skin. Instinctively, she turned to run, but it was no use. A hand shot out and grabbed her arm. A shrill cry escaped her lips before another hand cut it off, and bitter anger welled up inside her, which to her own astonishment was not directed toward the intruders as, logically, it should have been, but toward Langston instead. He had promised this sort of thing could not happen to her now, and despite all his silly precautions, it was happening! Where were his men? How had they let this happen? To her!

Struggling furiously with a strength fired by anger, she nearly broke free of her captor, but then he called out in a low voice, and she immediately sensed another body in front of her. She went still.

"Quite a little wildcat," the man holding her commented in an undertone.

"Well, she'll keep quiet if she knows what's good for her," growled the other. At that moment, Kendall was sure she heard a car door slam out in the street. The two men fell silent, and she tried to struggle again. "Bring her," ordered the second man in a harsh whisper. Kendall found herself being dragged toward the rear of the flagway. Then there was a little more light as they turned the corner into the yard.

She could make out their shapes now, one tall and wide-shouldered, the other like a barrel—or at least, that's what he felt like as he held her close against him. She couldn't really see any more than the shape of his head above hers as she twisted in his grasp.

They stopped just around the corner. They couldn't be seen by anyone coming through the gate, of course, because the guest cottage presented a solid black backdrop to the end of the walkway. The men holding her did not attempt to keep her from seeing who pushed the gate slowly open, and though she could only make out a shape as the opening widened, she knew instinctively that it was Steve, and she tried with all her might to break free, to warn him.

He paused in the opening. What if they had guns? What if they just shot him? He made the world's best target, just standing there like he was. Her stomach knotted up with nerve-shattering fear. What was the matter with him? He seemed to hesitate when she would have expected him to come storming up to the house, demanding that she let him in, that she have things out with him, or . . . or what? Her imagination boggled.

She heard him mutter something to himself. It sounded as though he was disgusted by something. Disgusted that the light was out after he had ordered that he be able to read fine print at midnight? With a little snort, he turned away and moved slowly, almost unsteadily, down the hill again, leaving the gate wide open behind him.

There was enough light on the street that she could see the shape of him moving away. Then there came the metallic sound of a car door opening, and the interior light in the Datsun flashed on, outlining him more distinctly. Her heart cried out to him, first to come and save her from the dreadful men, then to leave, to get away to safety in case he should be their actual target. He leaned into the car, seeming to search for something, and it quickly became obvious that he didn't mean to drive away. She had known he wouldn't. He wouldn't have left her gate open.

The man holding her whispered something, but she was concentrating too hard on Steve to pay any attention. Then the taller man said sharply, "Wait for him. He just forgot something."

Kendall shivered. It *was* Steve they wanted. They had probably meant to hold her as a hostage, demanding that he give himself or some piece of vital information up to them in exchange for her release. But this would be much better from their point of view. Now they would have both of them. If her presence didn't convince Steve to get them whatever they wanted, they could simply hold him until Langston Industries coughed up the goods. But would the company do that?

She was nearly as certain as she could be that Steve would not allow himself to be coerced by such tactics, and she would not put it past him to have left orders that Langston Industries was not to knuckle under to any terroristlike demands. If Sylvia were there and believed Steve's life to be in danger, she might defy those orders, but nobody else would dare. And Sylvia would be in Los Angeles until Wednesday at the earliest.

Steve was coming back. He still moved slowly. Just from the way he was walking, she knew he must be incredibly tired. Oh, why hadn't he stayed home in bed where he belonged!

"What's the matter with him?" demanded the man holding her in a guttural whisper.

"Dunno. Ask the chick." Cold steel nudged her under her chin, and Kendall felt her knees turn to putty. "Feel that, chicky?" She nodded, fear coursing through her. "That'll send you to the moon, chicky, if you so much as whimper. Is there something wrong with your lover boy?"

The hand lifted just enough to let her mutter, "He's been terribly ill. He . . . he shouldn't be out of bed yet."

"Good enough," the gravelly voice observed. "Won't put up much of a fight then."

Steve was once more approaching the gate. Kendall went absolutely still. If she could con the man who was holding her into thinking he had her completely under control, perhaps he would relax enough to let her break free. She didn't care what happened to her if she could just warn Steve. But the man did not relax, and Steve came through the gate. He dragged along as though he was in pain, and she wondered if the fever had stricken again. She railed at him inside her head. Stupid, stupid man! Go away. They're here, they're here!

But if he sensed anything out of the ordinary, he gave no sign of it as he slowly approached the door. He had left the gate ajar, no doubt either because he was too dazed to notice or because he needed the small amount of light that came through it to find his way to the doorstep. He reached the step, and she heard a light tap-tap on the door. The taller man slipped silently past her into the walkway. Steve knocked again, louder this time, and then she heard his voice.

"Kendall, it's me, Steve. Open up." He didn't sound sick, she thought. He sounded normal, not sick, not even angry. He sounded just as though he were paying an ordinary call. That was rather odd, she thought.

Steve began to knock harder. Then suddenly the knocking ceased altogether, rather abruptly, and she heard the tall man's voice. "That's enough, Langston. Just hold the racket down, and keep your hands where I can see 'em. That's it. Good boy. You packing a rod?"

"No, but I suppose you'll want to check that for yourself." Now she could hear the suppressed anger. She wondered if it was aimed at the men or at himself for allowing them to catch him off guard. A silence fell, and she supposed the tall man was searching Steve for a weapon. "Kendall? You there?"

The hand was still over her mouth, so she couldn't reply, but the tall man growled, "She's there all right, and if you cooperate with us, Langston, she just might get out of all this in one piece. And I hope," he added with a detectable sneer in his voice, "that you're not expecting reinforcements. We put your boys out of action for the time being. Good thing we chose the night we did to case the joint. Otherwise, we might have blown this little caper tonight. But, lucky for us, we got to see them in action."

Another shiver shot through Kendall's body as she realized that these must be the same two men who had passed by in the car while Jack was being pushed about by Langston's men. No wonder they hadn't responded to her frantic waving!

"Okay, he's clean. Bring the girl. She's got the key to the house, and I don't propose to spend the night out here."

The man holding her pushed Kendall forward, and she let herself stumble a bit, hoping that might make him relax his grip. But it didn't work. He merely snapped her upright again, grating a command that she watch her step. "Where's them keys, girl?" he asked. She shook her head. She really didn't know where they were. She had had them in her hand after she opened the gate, but she must have dropped them when they grabbed her.

He felt inside her jacket pockets, then in her shoulder bag, still holding his hand clamped across her mouth. "She musta dropped 'em, boss."

"Then they'll be near the gate. Take her with you and find them. If she opens her mouth, belt her."

"There's no need for that," Steve said in a calm voice. "I've got a key to the house. It's on my key ring. In the front pocket of my pants." He paused. "I'll get it if you like."

Kendall heard him, and despite the situation, she felt a sense of angry shock. He had a key to her house! Of all the nerve! She supposed his men must have made an extra one for him, and what Mr. Donnelly and friend had thought about that little request she didn't really want to contemplate. But the taller man interrupted her train of thought by ordering Langston to keep his hands right where they were.

"I even sense an odd move from you, buster, and the girl gets it right now. Understood?"

"Whatever you say. You seem to have the upper hand."

"You're right about that. Now, I'll get the keys. You just mind your p's and q's."

There was another silence, and then a split second before it happened, Kendall knew, as clearly as though he had told her, exactly what Steve meant to do. She braced herself, and sure enough, just as her nerves reached screaming pitch, there came the sudden sound of a scuffle, then a resounding crack of bone against bone, followed by the clank of metal striking cement.

The man holding her, caught entirely off guard by Steve's move, relaxed his hold for the brief second necessary for her to clamp her teeth down on his hand as hard as she could. He reacted instantaneously, yelping with pain and throwing her from him. Such was his strength that she spun away, completely unable to save herself before she crashed into the fence, the side of her head striking the heavy boards with a sickening thud. It seemed then as if the lights had come on in little sprinkles all around her, and she heard Steve's voice faintly, far off in the distance, before everything went black.

CHAPTER 11

The next conscious thought Kendall had was that she was floating up and up and up from a dense, cloying darkness toward a dim, faraway light. Somehow, she knew that if she struggled to reach the light, it would disappear, so she kept perfectly still, almost holding her breath. Exhaling would make her heavier, less buoyant, and would cause her to sink back into that awful darkness. She must make herself breathe lightly, must keep every muscle completely relaxed. She would not even think about trying to reach the light. She would just let her body float all by itself, and sooner or later, she would be able to breathe quite normally again. The dim gray light seemed to take on a golden warmth, then to grow a bit stronger. Her eyelids fluttered.

"Kendall! Come on, Kendall, snap out of it. Look at me." The familiar, compelling voice came from right over her head, and the anxiety in it sent a surge of vitality right through her weary body. Obediently, she made an effort to open her eyes, but the lids still felt extraordinarily heavy, and if she struggled, she knew the darkness would claim her again. "Open your eyes, Kendall," the persistent voice commanded. "Now, Kendall, right now! You can do it."

She could do it. The voice said so. Exerting all her will-power, she blinked. The warm golden light intensified. It came from the lamp beside the bed. She seemed to be lying in her own bed, as a matter of fact. That was confusing. Surely, she had been outside somewhere. And there had been men, bad men. And Steve. Her eyes focused on the ruggedly handsome face peering down anxiously into hers. "Steve," she whispered. Then her voice grew stronger as it took on an accusatory note. "So you really do have a key to my house!"

"No such luck," he retorted with a grin of undisguised relief. "I just needed to keep those lugs away from that gate." The rather cryptic statement seemed to make excellent sense to her, but when she tried to nod her head to show him that she understood, the room tilted crazily, then faded away into blackness again.

The next time there was no floating sensation. Instead, she was conscious of a murmur of voices, then a gentle pressure on one of her eyelids just before a blaze of light invaded that eye. She struggled to turn her head away.

"Easy, Kendall, you're all right now. Just let me do my job, will you?" At the sound of the gruff voice, she opened both eyes to discover that Steve had somehow managed to change into Dr. Weatherby. He was bending over her. Meg's worried voice sounded behind him.

"How is she?"

"Tell you for sure in a minute," he said shortly. The light flashed briefly, first in one eye, then in the other. "How's your head?" he asked.

Her mouth felt dry, but she could speak well enough. "It hurts."

"All over?"

She thought about it. "Sort of, but mostly on the left side I think. Where's Steve?"

"He had business to tend to," the doctor replied. "Don't know why he's not dead on his feet. Deserves to be. You've got a concussion," he pronounced, straightening up and slipping the penlight into his breast pocket. "Only a mild one, but you'll have to stay in bed for a few days. Got somebody who can take care of you?"

"Aunt Hilda will come," Meg declared. "Between us, we'll see that she behaves, Dr. Weatherby."

"Good enough. I'll check back tomorrow to see how she's doing, but there's no need to fret. Might be a good idea to wake her once in a while tonight, just to be on the safe side. I

won't give you any medication until tomorrow, young lady,"
he added, speaking directly to Kendall, "which means you'll
probably have the lulu of a headache all night, but it can't be
helped. We don't want to mask any symptoms, just in case
I've underestimated the thickness of your skull. You just try
to get as much sleep as you can. Best thing for you." He
patted her hand and was gone a moment later. Meg grinned
at her and pulled up a chair.

"How do you really feel?"

"Awful. What happened anyway? I remember Steve saying he had the keys to the house, and I remember biting that
awful man, but then the lights went out."

"Well, I don't know all the details, of course, but I do know
that they sent two men to the hospital. One has a broken jaw,
and they think the other one has serious internal injuries. I
think Steve must have been pretty mad." Kendall's eyes
widened.

"Was he hurt?"

Meg chuckled. "He hardly had a scratch on him, but he
was sure in a stew about you. He said he heard a loud crash
and called your name, but there was no answer, only this
huge body flying through the air at him. Said he had to
dispose of that little problem before he could find out what
had happened to you. His men were all over the place by
then though, and it wasn't long before the lights were up
again, but I can tell you, I never want to go through anything
like this again."

"I must have been out for quite a while," Kendall said.

"Only a few minutes. Steve's men took care of the bad guys
while he carried you in here, and I called Dr. Weatherby. He
lives right here in town, you know. Just a few blocks away,
actually. That's why he got here so fast."

"But what were you doing here?"

"I was having a cup of hot chocolate out on the front porch
with one of the men watching my cottage when the call
came to get over here on the double, so I followed them."
Kendall chuckled, sounding almost her normal self again,

and Meg spread her hands with a defensive grin. "Well, what do you expect? It nearly drove me nuts to think of those guys just sitting out there watching the house. They wouldn't both come up to the porch at the same time, of course, but I thought it ridiculous that they couldn't have something to keep them warm, at least."

"I don't think I'd mention it to Steve if I were you," Kendall said dryly.

"Don't worry. Even I've got better sense than that," Meg replied with a mock shudder. Then she grew serious. "Shouldn't you be trying to get some sleep?"

"Probably. I gather you plan to stay?"

"All night, my dear. I'll catnap in your guest room, but I promise to hear if you call out. And I'll check from time to time, too, just like the doctor ordered. I wonder what I'm supposed to do if I can't wake you."

Kendall smiled. "You'll think of something."

"Guess I will at that," Meg agreed. "Will that light bother you if I leave it on?"

Kendall managed to stop herself just short of shaking her aching head and said, "No. Good night, Meg."

But once she was alone, sleep seemed far away. Her head pounded miserably. When she tried to find a more comfortable position, she nearly made herself dizzy in the attempt. But then the pain dwindled into a measured throbbing, and she found that she could think again. She remembered the horrifying moment when she had feared that the men might kill Steve as he stood outlined at the gate. Then she remembered the way his voice had sounded, perfectly calm, as though the whole business were ordinary enough to be boring. Next came the memory of his face above hers as she floated to consciousness the first time. Her thoughts lingered there. In her mind's eye she studied him fondly, feature by feature.

He was the sort of man she had dreamed of but had never expected to meet, a sincere, strong, courageous man who would always make her proud of him. A handsome, truly masculine man with more thoughts in his head than she could uncover in a lifetime. He was never shallow, never weak or petty.

He would always dominate, and perhaps he would be a trifle more possessive than she liked her men to be, but she thought she could trust him to respect her independence, too. He wouldn't be like Jack and expect her to live only for him. He would allow her her moments of privacy, and she felt instinctively that he would provide the security she needed, the security she had nearly found with Meg's family but never with her own.

If someone had pointed out to her at that very moment that she had only known the man for a week, she would have scoffed at the absurdity of such a notion. She had known him all her life. Perhaps they had not met before, but she had recognized him at once. She had known. And she knew now that she would meet him on his own terms, whatever they were. If that was how the thing was meant to be, that's how it must be. And if it never led to anything more . . . Well, she would just have to deal with that circumstance when it happened.

Again, the vision of the man she loved standing outlined against the night sky, a perfect target, intruded. She shuddered, sickened by the thought of what had so nearly happened. No longer would she resist him. The matter was settled. Therefore, after a space of time that seemed only moments, when she realized that someone was roughly shaking her, it seemed perfectly natural when she opened her eyes to see Steve standing over her again.

"Hi," she said sleepily, smiling up at him. "What have you done with Meg?"

He grinned back at her. "I shut off her alarm. Weatherby tracked me down to give me the word about you, and I decided if you had to be wakened in the middle of the night, I'd prefer to do it myself."

"Why?"

"Just to be sure you're really all right," he replied gruffly. "You gave me quite a scare, sweetheart."

"Not by choice, believe me," she said huskily, hugging the endearment to herself. "Why did you come over when you did?"

"To see you," he replied simply. "I actually got here before you did, so I decided to check on my watchdogs while I waited. I didn't know exactly where they had hidden themselves, but I figured if I drove down the road slowly enough, somebody would recognize the car and show himself. Only nobody did, so I pulled in at the side of the road and got out to have a look. Found poor old Severson almost immediately. He was tied and gagged. Said somebody had jumped him. I got him free and, with his help, found his partner stuffed under a clump of oleanders. You must have driven in while we were looking, because the next time I looked, your car was in the carport. Scared me silly. I dashed for my car and told Severson to call in the boys at Meg's and wait for my signal."

"Signal?" She stared at him in momentary confusion before she realized what he must have done. "When you went back to the car?"

"Right. A hand radio. Figured I'd be the one person they wouldn't risk shooting. I hammed it up a bit, too. Thought they'd be more confident if I looked tired and decrepit."

"You *are* tired and decrepit," she said, trying to sound stern and failing completely. "You ought to be in bed yourself, you idiotic man, instead of here watching over me like some giant-sized mother hen."

"I wish you'd stop trying to make an invalid out of me," he retorted irritably. "I said I was fine, and I am. Now, do you want to hear the rest of this tale, or shall I clam up and order you back to sleep?"

"The rest, please," she said meekly.

"That's better. There really isn't much more. You know what happened up until the time that goon smacked you into the fence—at least, I assume you didn't walk into it by yourself." He paused with a teasing lift of an eyebrow, but she only smiled at him. He grinned back. "I've been waiting for that. Have you got any idea what sort of magical things a smile does to your face? All right, all right, don't wrinkle up at me. Where was I? Oh yeah, the goons. I wanted the one holding the gun on me to get close enough for me to deal with him. I'd thought I could manage it while he searched me for a weapon, but he was too careful. Then the bit about the keys came up, and I was afraid they'd see my men moving up on the house if they got too close to that gate, so I came up with my small inspiration. He let me turn around in order to look for what was supposedly in my pocket, and that's when the fun started. I guess Meg probably told you the rest."

"Enough," she agreed. "Who were they, Steve?"

"We aren't really sure," he replied. "We know they somehow found out enough about the project to know they could sell information about it, but they can't possibly be real professional types. They've made too many big mistakes. I'm not even sure what they hoped to accomplish by abducting you, except of course to try to force my hand. Even that wouldn't do them much good though. We have copies of the original plans plus most of the updates here at the main office, but the prototype of the gizmo itself is being constructed somewhere else, and it hasn't even been completed yet. Bits and pieces are located literally all over the world, and changes in the basic design are still being made constantly."

"Well, they certainly must have thought they could accomplish something."

"And that's what made them so dangerous. Guys like those two wouldn't have believed for a minute that it wasn't within our power to get them whatever it was they wanted."

She smiled at him again. "At least, now you can call off your watchdogs."

"Right, but not for the reason you think. I'm having you moved to the Sandcastle tomorrow, where you can be looked after properly."

"You are not!"

"I am. You can't stay here all by yourself, and there are people there who can take proper care of you. Besides, I'll be able to see for myself that you do what you need to do to get better quickly." He managed to keep his voice level, but Kendall could see the telltale indications of his rising temper and forced her own to stifle itself. She would get nowhere by fighting with him. Besides, she didn't think she was strong enough. In fact, she felt very, very tired.

It sounded in her voice. "Steve, I will not go to the Sandcastle, and you've got no right to demand it. Meg and Aunt Hilda will take very good care of me right here. It will only be for a couple of days. And it will do you no good to bluster or make ridiculous demands. No matter what you say, I simply won't go."

His color deepened, and he opened his mouth as though he meant to bluster and demand a good deal, but before he could get a single word out, he was interrupted by Meg's fierce voice from the doorway.

"And just what do you think you're doing here at this hour, Stephen Langston? Kendall is supposed to be getting as much sleep as possible, and you know perfectly well that you ought to be home doing exactly the same thing!"

"I slept till noon," he snapped. "And I intend to stay right here till morning."

"No, you will not. And there's not the slightest advantage to be gained by losing your temper with me either, because I've got two brothers who could run rings around you in that department, and I won't be the least bit impressed by one of your childish tantrums. Kendall won't sleep if you stay, and sleep she must. Besides that, you've got to go to your office tomorrow, so it would be altogether stupid for you to stay up all night." She jerked her thumb toward the hallway. "Now, out!"

Looking a little dazed, Langston got to his feet. He glanced at Kendall, then shot Meg a narrow look. "To think I've always thought of you as the harmless, friendly sort."

"That's me, sure enough," Meg agreed, grinning back at him. "A real puppy. But when I snap, I've got some pretty sharp teeth. So say good night, buster, and be on your merry way. I'll take good care of her."

"I'll go," he said slowly, "but don't think I've given up. She would be much more comfortable at the Sandcastle, and you both know it."

"Maybe, maybe not. But the matter is not open for debate right now."

Langston nodded, and a few moments later Meg had locked the front door and the gate behind him. She came back into the bedroom smiling. "That takes care of that. Hope you didn't mind me playing tigress in defense of her young."

"Not at all," Kendall replied. "It was probably good for him. Good night, Meg."

Alone again, she smiled at herself. So much for her decision to submit to whatever he asked of her. Clearly, making a decision and sticking to it were two entirely different things. There had been no way to avoid flaring up at his cool decision to remove her from her own house, however, and no doubt her reaction would be exactly the same any other time he tried to dictate to her in such a way. It was utterly hopeless to think she might be capable of simply lying down to let him walk over her. She wasn't made of such stuff as that. Never would she be someone else's doormat. She loved Steve Langston with all her heart, but no matter what sort of relationship developed between them in the future, it was perfectly obvious to the meanest intelligence that it would not be all clear sailing and sunny weather.

When she awoke late the next morning, it was to discover that Meg had gone to check things out at the studio, leaving Aunt Hilda to look after her. The older woman was clearly distressed by the events of the previous night, but she was constitutionally incapable of fuss, so she showed her concern by providing an excellent breakfast and her own good company.

When the doctor stopped by later in the morning, he declared Kendall to be out of the woods and left some medication to alleviate her headaches. Her first impulse was to get up, to do something constructive, but when she found that standing made her dizzy, she decided she might just as well stay in bed for the day.

The phone rang at three o'clock. She reached quickly for the receiver and realized when she heard Steve's voice on the line that she had been waiting for his call since the moment she had awakened.

"Kendall, I just called to be sure you were awake," he said crisply. "I'm on my way over right now. I've got that bill for Donnelly's services ready for you."

He hung up on her muttered response, and she put the phone slowly back in the cradle, conscious of a deep sense of depression. She glanced at Hilda, who was sitting placidly in the little slipper chair, an open magazine in her lap.

"That was Steve. He's coming over. Sounds like he's still pretty angry." She had told Hilda all about the events of the night before, including Meg's successful battle with Steve.

Hilda smiled now, comfortingly. "I'm sure he's just worried and thinks no one else can possibly take care of you as well as he can. He seems to be that sort of man."

Kendall agreed with her, but she could not help fearing that Steve was more than usually upset. He had sounded so cold, as though the only reason he was coming at all was to bring that horrid bill. How much would it be? She had been lamentably stubborn about that business, and now he was going to call her on it. It would probably take months to pay the thing off!

When he arrived, she was sitting up against a pile of pillows, her hair brushed, her makeup carefully applied, and wearing a frilly little pink bed jacket that Hilda had unearthed for her. Hilda let him in, and he strode directly into the bedroom with scarcely a word to her. But when she followed him, he turned after a brief, speculative glance at

Kendall and said coolly, "I'd like to be alone with her, if you don't mind."

Hilda raised an eyebrow in mock disapproval, but she voiced no objection when he firmly ushered her out of the room and shut the door behind her.

Kendall watched him warily. She was certain he was going to repeat his demand that she let him take her to the Sandcastle. Instead, he seemed to hesitate near the door, looking for a brief instant almost like a mischievous schoolboy. Then the look faded, to be replaced by one more anxious, and he visibly braced himself before he approached the bed, holding out an envelope.

"Here. You'd better open it."

His voice was carefully even. Reluctantly, she took the envelope and opened it, watching him. His attitude was bewildering, to say the least. Kendall continued to stare speculatively at him for a moment, the open envelope resting in her lap. Then her gaze lowered to the slip of yellow paper inside, and she drew it out slowly and turned it over. There were no figures, only two words scrawled across the center of the paper:

Marry me.

Eyes widening with astonishment, she seemed to freeze, almost afraid to look up, afraid to see by the expression in his eyes that he was joking, that there was some sort of mistake. He didn't want to marry her! She had been absolutely certain of that. But she could not deny herself the wonderful feelings that raced through her body as she stared at those two magical words. She would savor those feelings. She would not look up to have them dashed by—

"Well?" His voice sounded rough-edged, forced, unlike she had ever heard it before. She took a deep breath, still staring at the paper in her hand.

"Isn't . . ." She paused to clear her throat, then went on in a firmer voice. "Isn't this a rather drastic means of getting your own way?"

He was beside her instantly, his hands roughly on her

shoulders. "Stop staring at that damned thing and look at me. I've got to see what you're thinking, and the only way I can ever tell is when I can see your eyes." He sounded desperate, and her doubts evaporated into thin air. She looked up at him, and her eyes were shining. He relaxed. "Thank God. I was scared to death you wouldn't want to, and I'm not at all certain now that I could live without you. Oh, Kendall, I love you so much!"

A moment later, she had melted into his arms, and his lips claimed hers with a passion that sent shock waves pulsating through her. This was where she belonged, she thought ecstatically. She fit into his embrace as though she was meant to be there. She had come home. And Steve knew it. She could sense his confidence in the very way he kissed her, as though he would possess her. But there was gentleness, too. As a husband he would demand much, but he would give much in return. She might have to fight him at times for her independence, but he would make an effort to understand her needs and would give them as much consideration as he was capable of giving. She sighed, snuggling closer, and it was some time later before she could breathe properly again. By then he, too, was sitting back against her pillows, her head cradled gently against his shoulder. He looked down at her.

"Are you sure?"

"Positive," she said happily. "I've always loved you. I knew it the first time I looked into your eyes."

"That's funny," he grinned. "The first time I looked into yours, something frightened the wits out of me. I think that's why I was so edgy. I knew I wanted you days ago. Never gave much thought to marriage though. Didn't think I'd have time for it. But the moment I found you all crumpled up by that fence, I knew I could never let you go. You need me, and I couldn't bear the thought that you might let some other guy take care of you."

"It isn't necessary to marry me," Kendall found herself saying. "I'd already decided before you got here to be whatever you wanted me to be."

His voice sharpened. "No. We'll do the thing all legal and proper, and we'll have a zillion kids, and a collie and kittens and whatever else goes with the territory. Would you mind terribly if I asked you to stop working?"

"Not terribly," she admitted. "I'd want to keep my hand in, I think, but I could easily retain my share of the partnership and train someone else to do what I do. With all the business we've been getting, we'll have to hire some more people sooner or later, anyway."

"I suppose that would do," he agreed with a crooked smile. "But when I have to take off for Timbuktu, I want my wife to go with me whenever it's feasible. Deal?"

"Deal." She put out her hand and solemnly shook his. "But will you have to go to Timbuktu often?"

"Not often. I think it's time I started giving Sylvia more responsibility."

"She'll like that, I think," Kendall said. "While you were delirious, you said something about not doing the job properly, and she thought you meant her. Said she'd prove she could do the thing right while she was in L.A."

Steve frowned. "Can't imagine what I was babbling about, but it wasn't Sylvia. I was probably worried about myself, not her. More than likely, I was babbling about not being able to take care of you properly. Sylvia can be downright officious at times, but she does a terrific job, and I don't know where I'd be without her. It's definitely time to let her spread her wings a bit more. We're going to need a honeymoon, after all."

Kendall chuckled, but then a new thought struck her, and her expression grew serious again. "Will we have to take bodyguards on the honeymoon?" she asked.

With a laugh, he hugged her. "That still rankles, doesn't it, sweetheart?" She wriggled against him, not wanting to admit it but unable to suppress her feelings entirely. He only hugged her more tightly. "You'll have to get used to it just as I have. It's a sort of dues I pay for being privileged enough to do as I like with my life."

"I suppose, put like that, it makes *some* sense," she agreed doubtfully. "But you didn't really answer my question."

"Bodyguards on our honeymoon?" He grinned down at her. "Aren't you the same girl who said that if she had something worth protecting she'd put on a grand display with fences, guards, dogs . . . the works?"

"I wasn't talking about people!"

"But you, my precious girl, are worth far more to me than any government gizmo could ever be," he retorted in a voice ringing with sincerity. He took her chin firmly in hand and turned her face up to his. For a moment, there was no opportunity for further conversation.

When she could speak, Kendall said a bit breathlessly, but with resignation as well, "I suppose the watchdogs—human or otherwise—are necessary."

Steve chuckled. "You'll hardly know they're around, I promise. And when we get back, you'll be too busy. I guess you and Meg will have to make a few changes in the plans for the house now. We're no longer concerned with only my colors after all. What season are you?"

"Winter," she replied. Then she laughed. "I think I've already been planning, although I certainly would have denied it if Meg had been tactless enough to make the accusation." She told him about her suggestions for living-room accessories and the swatches for the study drapes. He grinned sagely, and she wrinkled her nose at him, saying sternly, "Well, it's a good thing our colors are compatible. It will be much easier to make adjustments than it would be if I were autumn or spring!"

"You can tell me all about it on our honeymoon," Steve said with a look that spoke even more strongly than his words had of his love for her. "I was thinking of Paris or London, but I think now that it will have to be Omaha. Once we've toured the cornfields, the old stockyards, and the Strategic Air Command's headquarters, there will be nothing else to see and nothing to do. We'll be forced to fall back on our own resources for something to occupy our time. I think I'd like that best of all."

Kendall grinned at him. Then, giving a long sigh, she snuggled back against his shoulder with a sense of warmth and well-being, the sort of feeling that only comes with the delicious security of love. By the time Hilda silently opened the door to be sure everything was all right, Kendall was sound asleep, held gently in Steve's arms. He had been watching her contentedly, but the movement of the door caught his attention. He looked up at Hilda and winked.